ALICE
THROUGH THE NEEDLE'S EYE

ALICE
THROUGH THE NEEDLE'S EYE

BY

GILBERT ADAIR

WITH TWENTY-TWO ILLUSTRATIONS BY
JENNY THORNE

MACMILLAN

FOR ELIZABETH MARY ELLIOT

First published 1984 by
MACMILLAN CHILDREN'S BOOKS
A division of Macmillan Publishers Limited
London and Basingstoke.
Associated companies throughout the world

British Library Cataloguing in Publication Data
Adair, Gilbert
  Alice through the needle's eye.
  I. Title
  823'.914 [J]   PZ7

ISBN 0 333 37361–8

Designed by Philip Miles.
Phototypeset by Wyvern Typesetting Limited, Bristol.
Printed in Hong Kong.

CONTENTS

CHAPTER I

A NEEDLE IN A HAYSTACK

Even if Alice didn't know for certain how long she had been trying to thread the needle, she couldn't help but notice that the sand in the hour-glass which stood on the chimney-piece was slipping away at an alarming rate. "If I don't succeed *very* soon," she thought "poor Dinah's jacket wo'n't be ready till next winter but one!"

Dinah was the cat, now quite old and sleepy. As her mistress liked to boast to whoever would listen to her, she had had as many as, oh, *ump*teen kittens, perhaps even twice that mysterious number. (For Alice, no matter how slowly and carefully she counted, somehow never managed to find a place for umpteen, "though I can certainly count up to twenty, and umpteen *must* come before that.") Now the kittens had kittens of their own. "What ought one to call *them*, I wonder? Grand-kittens?" Yes, thought Alice with a dreamy smile, the word would do nicely. For hadn't they all been grand kittens, every last fluffy one of them, and hadn't she grieved when – such is the destiny of kittens – they had been given away, one by one, to those friends of hers who were allowed to offer them a home?

To return to Dinah, however, she would shiver so in winter: and to-day, cold and Decemberish, she was already curled up, as tight as a ball of wool, on the rug directly in front of the blazing fire. So Alice had decided at last to sew back on the button missing from Dinah's snug little woollen jacket, which her sister (Alice's, that is, not Dinah's) had knitted many winters ago. But she still hadn't completed the all-important task of thread-ing the needle.

Presently, after taking aim, she tried again – and again she missed. "Really, it's the vexingest thing!" cried Alice, sucking furiously on the limp end of the thread. "Why, if only I'd had the common sense to put the needle *here* – " (moving it ever so slightly over to the right) " – the thread would have gone through with room to spare!" She glared at both the needle and thread with as stern an expression as she could muster at such short notice. "Oh, do open your eye a bit wider, for goodness' sake," she addressed the needle crossly, "otherwise we'll be here all day!" (though, being a very fair little girl, Alice was honest enough to admit that, if someone were to shove a piece of thread into *her* eye, she would most probably want to close it altogether); and to the thread, in an excellent likeness of how her nurse sometimes spoke to her, she said, "Stand up straight – head high – no slouching, *please!*"

Then, more determined than ever, Alice slowly edged the end of the thread closer and closer to the needle's eye; and this time, right up to the very last, she hadn't the slightest doubt that it was going to pass through. But, just when success seemed about to crown all her efforts, the thread stopped and quivered – exactly as if it were wrinkling up its nose (as Alice fancied) – before twisting off provokingly to the *left* side. "Oh dear," she sighed, "I *knew* I should have left it where it was in the first place!"

All the afternoon it had been the same story. It seemed that, wherever Alice chose to hold the needle, the thread would happily have gone through *the time before* or *the time after* – but never at the right time.

Alice flung down the needle and thread in exaspera-
tion. She too would have liked to curl up in front of the
fire, as she was quite tired out by so much hard work.
And thinking about hard work led her naturally (can
you see why?) to think of the Aardvark, which, as it
happened, was the very first word in the big dictionary
that she had fetched down from the library that morning
to study. Alice, you see, had made up her mind to
improve her conversation by learning one new word by
heart every day; and since there's no amusement to be
had by learning anything on one's own, she decided (not
very seriously, though) to try and teach Dinah at the
same time, "that we might have some pleasant little
discussions together. But what a queer dictionary," she
said, half to Dinah and half to herself, "that starts with
the hardest and most useless word you could think of!"

So, thinking it would be better to lead off with a much
simpler lesson, Alice hunted out the first reading-book
she had ever owned, and began to repeat over and over
to Dinah "The cat sat on the mat", which appeared to
be the *whole* of Chapter I. Dinah, however, displayed no
more curiosity about it than about the Aardvark, "and
that's quite understandable," said Alice, stroking her,
"because sitting on a mat is the thing you do best in the

world, and what is the use of *reading* about something you can *do* just as well?"

Then she remembered that it was necessary to learn what sounds letters made before trying to compose words, and she knelt down close to Dinah's face and proceeded to recite the alphabet to her: and here, she told herself, she did make *some* headway. Clever Dinah mastered the vowels in no time at all – for, even if they came out in a tumble, and Alice couldn't be certain she heard each one distinctly, Dinah's maeiou-ing never failed to put them in the correct order. The consonants proved much harder, except for 'm', and a *very* pronounced 's' whenever Alice tweaked her tail: but she wasn't at all discouraged, and decided that they would tackle 'b', 'c' and 'd' the first thing next morning.

"Yes, my dear," she said to Dinah, who hadn't stirred from the hearth, "I know how exhausting it is, but just think how nice it would be if we could chatter away merrily, you and I! There are so many things I'm dying to tell you – such as which birds you may eat in the garden, and which you may *not*, and what the French is for mouse, you know, and how many pecks make a bushel, all kinds of facts that may come in useful one day. And you must have lots to tell me, too – what it's like to have whiskers and a tail, and which was your favourite grandkitten – it was Buttercup, I'm sure, but I'd like to hear it from the cat's mouth – and when you're hungry, or thirsty, or not warm enough – "

At this Alice broke off, for she realised that she still had not sewn the button on Dinah's winter jacket. Wearily, she took up the needle and thread again, and set about the task. But this time, bringing the needle right up to her eyes, and half closing them, she was astonished to find herself peering – through *its* eye – at the most delightful little vista (and it *was* very little) you could ever imagine! Alice blinked, and looked again. There, as if it were carved on a cameo brooch, was a little yellow-green field, bordered by hedgerows and criss-crossed by what appeared to be tiny haystacks: it sloped gently down towards a sandy beach that stretched away to the horizon.

After her initial surprise, Alice was much less alarmed than she ought to have been, and she longed to wander across the field and walk barefoot along the shore. And whether the needle grew larger or Alice grew smaller, I cannot say – but, the next thing she knew, she was able to stick her head through as easily as if the needle's eye were a large open window. Her shoulders

followed soon after, so that the whole countryside was laid out beneath her, looking, she thought, with its green patches and winding lines, "more like the map of a country than the country itself." And just a moment later, leaning out a few inches too far, Alice lost her balance and toppled over.

One minute lazily playing with Dinah in front of a roaring fire, and in the next Alice found herself sailing through the sky on a bright summer's day! She was too interested in her new surroundings, however, to be really afraid, and she seemed to have all the time in the world to study them thoroughly. "I daresay," she thought, "this is what is meant by a bird's-eye view – and since I must be the only person who can ever have known what it's like, no doubt I'll be consulted as the leading expert on the subject – an Orni-theologist, I think it's called – " (she *thought*, but she was by no means *certain*) " – and how very odd that I should feel so safe up here when, actually, it ought to be rather dangerous for a little girl to be flying through the air."

As she fell, her body would sometimes turn upside-down, so that earth and sky changed place, and the neatly tilled field seemed to hover high above her head. "What a curious adventure this is, to be sure!" said Alice. "I'm certain I must be breaking the Law of Gravity: for, if I remember my lesson, it states that what goes up must come down – yet here am I clearly coming down – " (and though she was too busy thinking about what had happened to her to pay proper attention, Alice was beginning to come down a little more quickly than before) " – without ever having gone up. Unless sitting in an armchair can be considered *up* – which it is for Dinah, of course, but surely not for me. After all, I always say I'm going to sit *down*," she went on, adding thoughtfully, "though sometimes I'm *told* to sit *up*."

A moment later, Alice's eye was caught by a tiny object which suddenly glinted in the sunlight quite close to her. "What in the world can that be?" she cried. "An insect – a firefly, perhaps – why, there it goes again!" This time she succeeded in taking a good look at it, and discovered that it was none other than her needle, "which must have passed through its own eye, like a serpent swallowing its tail." Alice stretched out her hand to try and grasp it: all that happened, however, was that her whole body turned over 180 degrees, and she found that she was raising her arm just when she ought to have been lowering it. "Now what's to become of me?" she wondered, as the needle slipped away out of her reach. "I'll never be able to find my way back without it. And Dinah'll be getting quite anxious – at least, I think she will – and it's almost time for tea – that's to say, it *was* almost time: with everything so confused, I'm not at all certain it is any longer. We were going to have hot mince pies, as I remember, and there's nothing I like better on a cold December day – "

Here Alice broke off in puzzlement as, where she was now, it was far too warm for mince pies: and she was just trying to make up her mind what she *did* feel like, when suddenly there was no more time to think about such trivial matters, since the ground was rushing up to meet her at a frightening speed. Before she could utter another syllable, she had tumbled headlong into one of the haystacks.

Alice quickly recovered from the shock – only to

discover that, except for a pale ray of light above her head, it was pitch dark all around her. "Why, I must be *inside* the haystack!" she exclaimed. "Yes, I can feel wisps of tangled hay in my hair, and slipping under my collar and stockings – and very ticklish it is, too!" Sitting on the cold matted earth, with a wall of hay surrounding her, she decided that the first thing to be done was to find a way out. Upwards or outwards? With difficulty, she struggled to her feet, until she was standing at her full height; and to her relief she found that, in this position, her head comfortably cleared the top of the haystack, "though I must look as if I were going to a fancy-dress party."

She was wondering how best to free herself altogether, when she became aware of a faint squeaking just below her left ear. Since she couldn't turn her head to see where it came from without removing her ear from the vicinity of the noise, and she already had to strain to hear it, she stayed perfectly still for a moment or two and listened with all her might. And what she heard sounded remarkably like " 'Elp! 'Elp! Oh, somebody do 'elp me!", in the most mournful tone imaginable.

Alice felt she simply had to find out who or what was offering up such piteous pleas for help: and turning very slowly (not only because she was up to her neck in hay but also because she didn't want to alarm the creature more than she need), she was surprised to see what looked like a Country Mouse backing away from her as far as it could go without toppling off the haystack. Actually, it not only looked like a Country Mouse, it was one, save that it wore a little straw hat tilted over what, in a human being, would be called its brow: and it had recently been sucking on a short straw, which the chattering of its teeth was now causing to swing up and down in a comical manner.

Startled by the sight of Alice's face towering over it, the Country Mouse continued to scream " 'Elp!" more and more loudly, till it was almost as loud as you or me whispering. And when Alice saw it teeter dangerously on the very edge of the haystack, so that there seemed every possibility of its falling over, she was tempted to pick it up and set it down firmly again beside her: but her arms were so tightly wedged she could scarcely move them, "and it's just as well," she said to herself, smiling at her own joke, "for if I *did* try to pick it up, in the state it's in, that would be the last *straw*!"

Alice's smile, usually well appreciated, appeared not to calm the Country Mouse. "Oh, 'Eaven protect us!" it began to squeak in terror: "now it's a-cracking up!"

She looked down kindly at the poor animal. "If you please, Mr. Mouse," she addressed it in her gentlest voice, "I am *not* cracking up."

"Now it's a-roaring and a-bellowing after me! Oh, 'elp, 'elp!" cried the Mouse, which had turned quite pale.

"Why, I'm not bellowing at all," objected Alice. "I'm speaking just as softly as I can. Only you're so small by comparison, it must sound like bellowing to you."

At this the Mouse's nostrils quivered and its eyes narrowed, as if the opportunity of making a good point in an argument had caused it for the moment to forget why it ought to be afraid.

"Well now – if I *was* to h'accept that," it replied, after some reflection on the matter, "for the sake of the h'argument, mind you – it still don't seem fit be'aviour for a comet, now do it?"

Alice could hardly keep from laughing out loud. "No, it don't – I mean, it doesn't," she agreed, "except that I'm not a comet, you see, even though I *did* fall out of the sky like one. My name is Alice and – "

"Just what I thought," the Mouse nodded sagely: " 'Alley's Comet. You're early, though. You wasn't due – " (to Alice's astonishment, it pulled out a tiny Almanac from beneath its hat and began to study it intently) " – for another thirty-four years, seven months and thirteen days – *at least*. Not a word 'ere about you talking, neither. What *is* the universe a-coming to, I'd like to know!"

"I should look less like a comet," said Alice (who hoped she didn't look like one at all), "if the rest of me weren't buried under this haystack. But, really, I'm a little girl, so it's normal for me to be speaking. You speak extremely well yourself – " Alice was going to add " – for a Country Mouse", but since the Mouse seemed to have overcome its fear of her, and was calmly sucking on the wisp of straw, she quickly checked herself.

"Now that's because – " said the Mouse, carefully replacing the Almanac under its hat, " – I didn't h'always reside on a haystack."

"Where did you live before?" said Alice.

"In Threadneedle Street," said the Mouse, "right in the sound of Bow Bells. But what with us being as poor as church-wardens, as ye might say, and those Bells a-ringing in our ears all the day long, I h'upped and left, I did – changed places with a cousin of mine who 'oped to make 'is fortune in the City."

"And did he?" Alice asked, with much curiosity.

"Not 'e," said the Mouse complacently: "on account of the bulls and bears, you know."

Alice nodded, for she remembered hearing about such Bull and Bear Markets.

" 'Course," the Mouse went on, lowering its voice as if to impart a tremendous secret, even though Alice had difficulty at the best of times to make out what it was saying, "life 'ereabouts ain't a round of beer and skittles. Dear me, no! No bulls to speak of, nor bears neither, but there *are* stalks and shears – nasty, sharp, gilt-edged things, shears" – and a shudder ran through the Mouse at the very thought of them.

"I notice there are a great many bumble-bees as well," remarked Alice, who for some time had been troubled by them buzzing around, dreadfully close to her face. They were particularly worrying as she was unable to ward them off with her hands, which were still inside the haystack; and when one of them seemed about to settle on her nose, she felt she could not remain as she was an instant longer. Though it took a good deal of wriggling and a mighty flurry of hay, she managed to free her arms at last and wave the insect away.

Since the effect of this on the Mouse was to set it

trembling once more, and their conversation had been progressing quite pleasantly up to then, Alice was at pains to soothe its ruffled feelings.

"Oh, *dear* Mr. Mouse, I didn't mean to frighten you again," she began in the merest whisper, patting down the top of the haystack as she spoke till it was as flat and even as before, "but I simply had to make myself more comfortable."

"I never knew such a comet for wiggling and wriggling," said the Mouse in a crotchety voice: "and why you 'ad to choose *my* haystack to fall into – "

Alice was just about to insist that, for one thing, she was *not* a comet and, for another, she certainly hadn't *chosen* to fall into this or any other haystack, when she suddenly made out what it was in the Mouse's speech (apart from its being able to speak at all) that was puzzling her so: and, before she could stop herself, she blurted out, "How is it that you say ' 'ad' instead of 'had' and ' 'oped' instead of 'hoped', just like the road-sweeper does, yet you always manage to pronounce 'haystack' correctly – " Whereupon, realising at the very moment she uttered it that such a remark was *extremely* rude, she clapped both hands over her mouth.

The Mouse drew itself up with a pained expression.

"Oh, I could bite out my tongue!" exclaimed Alice, blushing. "I didn't intend to – I mean – only it *did* strike me – as strange, you know, and – "

"There ain't nothing strange about it," sniffed the Mouse, "because this ain't an 'aystack, you see. It's a haystack."

"I beg your pardon," said Alice politely.

"A haystack," the Mouse repeated, adding ungraciously, " – oh, see for yourself."

Though Alice didn't really understand what she was expected to find there, she dutifully took a closer look at the haystack: and, indeed, there *did* seem to be something unusual about its tangled surface. She picked up a wisp of hay, examined it thoroughly, and discovered that it was *very* queerly shaped. "Why, it's in the form of a capital A," she said to herself, turning it every which way. Alice picked up another, then a third. All were capital A's.

"What I told you," said the Mouse: "it's a h'A-stack."

"But whatever is it for?" asked Alice.

"You *are* slow," said the Mouse contemptuously. "This is where letters are 'arvested. Principal product 'ereabouts, letters are."

That was such a novel idea to Alice that she needed a

little time to think it over before asking at last, "And when is the harvest brought in?"

"Well, I ca'n't rightly speak for all the h'alphabet," said the Mouse, scratching its ear with the straw, "but it's best to make A's while the sun shines."

"Ye-es, I believe I have heard *something* of the sort," said Alice thoughtfully, brushing off a bee that was hovering too close for comfort. "Oh, bother them!"

"I should 'ope you wouldn't!" exclaimed the Mouse with indignation. "It ain't proper to go a-bothering bees at work."

"At work?" Alice repeated in a perplexed voice. "But surely bees' work is collecting pollen from flowers?"

" '*Er*eabouts," replied the Mouse (and it stressed the first syllable, as if to suggest that queer goings-on elsewhere were scarcely *its* concern), "they collect letters. To spell out words, you know. That's why they're called spelling bees."

Intrigued by this new piece of information, Alice was on the point of inquiring what it was they did with the completed words, when she noticed, just beneath her chin, a wisp of hay that didn't look quite right. Carefully picking it up between her thumb and her index finger, she discovered that it wasn't an A at all but an H.

At the sight of this, the Mouse's face took on such a woebegone expression that it was all Alice could do to turn her burst of laughter into a cough.

"Oh dear – oh deary, deary me!" it wailed. "There I go again – a-dropping my aitches where I shouldn't! I'll lose my place, you see if I don't – such a soft, cushiony place too!"

Alice was so taken aback by the Mouse's sorry state (for it did seem to take the matter awfully seriously), that she at once determined to be of what help she could.

"Why, Mr. Mouse, if what's making you unhappy is that it's the wrong letter," she said reassuringly, "I can mend that in no time."

Clasping the letter by its topmost ends, yet taking care not to break them, Alice bent them forward till they were touching at an acute angle – then she twisted the points together to form a knot, and the trick was done: the offending H had been turned into an A.

"There," she said, inspecting her handiwork with satisfaction: "I'm sure nobody'll be able to tell the difference."

The Mouse had been watching her efforts anxiously, and a little suspiciously: but now that it could see what she had achieved in so short a time, it actually managed to look quite sheepish. (Have you ever seen a *Mouse* looking *sheep*ish?)

"I thank ye," it said rather grudgingly. "For a comet that comes a-dropping on one's 'ead – " ("Mind those aitches," thought Alice) " – without so much as a by-your-leave, you could be worse, after all."

"Thank *you*," replied Alice. "But I do wish you'd stop calling me a comet. Haven't I already told you I – "

"Hush, comet!" said the Mouse. " 'Course that's what you are! Ain't nothing to be h'ashamed of, neither – a wondrous place the world would be if everybody could be a mouse, now wouldn't it?"

Though Alice doubted whether *she* would have called

it wondrous, she had to agree with the general drift of this last remark.

"And I good as guessed you was a-coming," the Mouse went on, "along of the particle that broke off you."

At first, Alice couldn't make out at all what it meant, as she hadn't dropped anything in her descent (and she was positive no part of *her* had broken off). Then she thought that the Mouse must be referring to her needle, which (you remember) had slipped past as she fell.

"Excuse me," said Alice, "but I really am very eager to hear what happened to that particle, as you call it – was it by any chance bright and silvery, with a sharp point at one end?"

"Might 'ave been," said the Mouse, displaying little enough interest in the subject. "All I know is, it near split me in two."

"Why, that was it, I'm sure," said Alice excitedly (thinking the while, "How it *does* exaggerate!"), and she began to delve into the haystack with both hands.

" 'Ave a care!" squeaked the Mouse. "Don't go a-turning everything 'iggledy-piggledy again, now we got it so neat. What *is* it you're about?"

"I'm looking for my needle," explained Alice, trying

to search with the least possible fuss. "You see, this whole adventure of mine really started when I was sewing on a button for – for Dinah, you know – " (for she half remembered trying out the word 'cat' on mice before, and finding them as little fond of it as of the animal itself) " – and somehow I managed to fall through the eye of the needle – "

"There ain't no 'i' in 'needle'," said the Mouse, whose voice was beginning to fade away altogether, "and you ain't as clever as you look."

Though Alice considered this rather offensive, she consoled herself with the thought that the Mouse at least recognised that she *looked* clever; and, for the moment, she was far too preoccupied with finding her needle to prove – by reciting a few Multiplication-Tables, for example – just how intelligent she was for her age. "But, oh, I'd like to know how I'm ever going to find a needle in a haystack," she said to herself. "It's exactly like – like looking for a – for a – "

Alice did not have time to complete her sentence, however, for half-way through it she spied the needle directly in front of her, and with a cry she held it up in the sunlight.

"Gracious, that wasn't nearly as hard as I thought it

would be!" she said delightedly. "And now that I've found it again, I can go back home by the same way, and see Dinah, and the tea-things mayn't have been cleared away yet. I'm certain all I have to do is bring the needle's eye alongside *mine* and – and yet – and yet – it *does* seem such a pity to be leaving so soon, when I haven't properly explored that little sandy beach down there. I so *very* much want to! Perhaps if I were to take a stroll down to it – and when I've walked around, and seen everything there is to see, *then* I can think of returning."

Alice was on the point of wishing the Country Mouse good-bye, and pondering how she might untangle herself from the haystack without causing another commotion, when she realised to her surprise that, while she had been letting her mind wander thus, both Mouse and haystack had vanished, and she was standing all alone in the middle of the field. To be sure, there *were* a few strands of hay clinging to her clothes and hair, but they were of the ordinary variety, and she quickly brushed them off.

"I wonder –" she began to say: then, without thinking any further on the question, she started running across the field to the beach beyond, which looked more inviting with every step she took.

CHAPTER II

A TALE WITH NO END

When Alice arrived on the shore, it was quite deserted; and though she couldn't say exactly what she had hoped to find there, it was a trifle disappointing to be walking over such beautiful runny sand without anybody to talk to – or play hand-ball with – or race into the sea with (which would have been an *extremely* long race, as the beach seemed to stretch away for miles and miles, with only a faint blue shimmer on the horizon to indicate that there *was* any sea at the end of it). Half-heartedly, she started to build a sand-castle, but decided it was too difficult without either a spade or pail. Then, when she tried to dig a large hole with her hands, no matter how far she scooped the sand, it would always manage to trickle back in again; so that, after several minutes of very tiring work, the place in front of her looked just as flat as the rest of the beach.

"Really, I ca'n't see what use a beach is," complained Alice, "if there are no star-fish, or bathing-huts, or lodging-houses on the promenade – one may as well take one's holiday in the Sahara Desert, for all the fun there's to be had!" She found so little to occupy herself with, that she was soon ready to turn back – "and at least I sha'n't have to change into dry clothes, or shake the sand out of my stockings, or anything like that" – when something soft and furry rubbed against her leg. Looking down, she discovered a Cat – no, there were *two* Cats, absolutely alike in every respect, weaving in and out between her ankles, when it was not between each other.

"Now where did *you* spring from, you darlings?" said Alice tenderly, kneeling to stroke them.

But before she could, the Cat at her left arched its back, and said in a high, piercing voice, "I declare! It speaks – and I imagined – "

" – it was only in fairy-tales – " continued the Cat at her right.

" – that human beings could speak," said the first Cat, abruptly ending the sentence.

Alice had never heard such a queer style of speaking before, and she let out a little cry. "Oh – you made me start!"

"Start *what*?" asked the second Cat.

"Why – just start," said Alice.

"Where I come from – " began the first Cat, causing Alice now to turn in *its* direction.

" – you have to start *something*," the second chimed in.

"Most anything'll do, you know," the first whispered helpfully in her ear; and they both fell silent as before.

"Oh dear," thought Alice, "a conversation with them is going to be *very* awkward!"

By now the Cats had come out from between her ankles, and she could see that they were actually joined together at the tails (or rather, tail, for there *was* only the one, you understand). And when she thought of the ease with which they had been curling round her legs, she couldn't imagine at all how they had succeeded without getting tangled in a painful knot.

"I don't mean to be personal," she timidly addressed the first one, "but I've never seen Cats – that's to say, a

Cat – no, I mean, two Cats joined at the middle before. What is the name of your breed, please?"

"If you *must* know – " said the *second* Cat. ("Oh, it's too bad!" sighed Alice. "I shall never get the hang of it.")

" – we're Siamese – " said the first Cat.

"Oh, but surely not," Alice interjected, for she prided herself on knowing a thing or two about this particular subject. "Siamese Cats are much smaller, you see, and they're yellowish-brown in colour, and they have blue eyes, whereas – "

" – *Twin Cats* – " the second came back, glaring at her.

" – was what I was *going* to say – " the first went on.

" – before I was so rudely – " said the second Cat.

" – so very, *very* rudely – " said the first Cat.

" – interrupted!" said the second Cat.

Since Alice had now lost count of which Cat she had offended, she decided to apologise to both of them at once.

"No offence taken," they answered this time in unison, "and none intended, we're sure."

Alice was relieved that her excuses had been so readily accepted, and she tried to remember if she had ever heard of Siamese-Twin Cats before. The name struck her as quite a logical one, "for, after all, even if they don't look Siamese," she said to herself, "it *is* true that Siamese-Twins are joined together, so I suppose that's why they were named after them."

"Not a bit of it!" said the first Cat, with a toss of its head.

"I beg your pardon?" said Alice, who hadn't realised that she had been thinking out loud.

Naturally, it was the second Cat's turn to speak. "It isn't at all how we got our name."

"In fact," said the first, "Siamese-Twins were named after *us*."

"Now I really don't understand," said Alice.

With a withering look, the second Cat began to address her as if to a child (which she *was*, of course, except that it must be a very disagreeable feeling to be talked down to by a Cat). "You would agree, I hope – "

" – that *it*'s as large as I am – " the first Cat went on, pointing at its twin.

"Why, yes," Alice began, "I should – "

"– and *it*'s as intelligent as I am – " said the second Cat (and so on, as before).

"As to that," Alice tried to reply, "I'm not – "

" – and as proud as I am – "

" – and as strong as I am – "

" – and as graceful as I am – "

" – and as cunning as I am – "

And so it went on, until Alice felt herself becoming giddier and giddier, and all she heard was a series of

" – as I am – "

" – as I am – "

" – as I am – "

" – as I am – "

Faster and faster they went, circling round her, and now Alice was able to catch just the tail, so to speak, of each phrase.

" – 's I am – "

" – 's I am – "

" – 's I am – "

" – 's I am – "

" – 's I am – "

" – 's I am – "

Then, just when she believed her head would spin off altogether, and roll along the shore like a top, the two Cats came to a sudden stop. Beaming triumphantly at Alice, they concluded as with one voice, "*That*'s why we're called *Siam*ese-Twin Cats!"

Alice took a minute to recover her breath. Then she decided that she would name them Ping and Pang – "it sounds quite Siamese, and it'll help me make out one from the other," she said to herself, "for Ping must always be at the left of the hyphen – I mean, the tail – and Pang at the right." So, addressing Ping, then hastily turning her attention to Pang, she asked, "Do you always speak like that – both together?"

"Always," replied Pang (and Alice smiled to herself, for having got it right at last).

"Why, we even laugh – "

" – and cry – "

" – together."

"Care for a demonstration?"

"Very much," said Alice respectfully, though she was strongly inclined to laugh herself, they were so solemn about it.

"Then you must tell us a joke – "

" – and as there are *two* of us – "

" – you'll have to make it *twice* as funny in the telling."

"Oh dear," said Alice uncertainly, "I'm afraid I ca'n't remember *any* jokes just at the present. Would a

riddle do? I know one that made *me* laugh ever so much."

"Proceed, child," said Pang, in a tone of profound melancholy.

"The answer's really quite simple," said Alice: "only rather hard to think of, you know." She nervously cleared her throat. "What kind of man is it that has a hat, a carrot, and three pieces of coal?"

As if plunged deep in thought, the two Cats started to pace back and forth on the shore, their tail making a funny little squiggle whenever they crossed each other's path. Only an occasional "Hum!" could be heard to suggest they were still attending to the riddle.

After three or four such "Hums", Ping turned to Alice and asked, "Are we getting warm?"

"I very much doubt it," she replied with a smile. "In order to get warm, you see, you must ask some questions."

"Well!" said Pang in astonishment, "I've heard some ways of getting warm – "

" – but *never* simply by asking questions."

"What a saving of fuel we'll have next winter!"

"However – " continued Ping.

" – as it's already *quite* warm enough to-day – "

" – and it might be unhealthy to go on – "

" – we give it up."

And they both looked expectantly at her.

"Oh, wouldn't you like to try a tiny bit harder?" pleaded Alice, who remembered that *she* had taken what seemed like hours to guess the solution. But since there was no response from either Cat, she took a deep breath, and said, "The answer is – a *snow*man!"

There followed such a long, such a deafening silence that Alice was beginning to wish the sand would open up and swallow her at once, when she heard a sound – a wonderfully small sound, to be sure, somewhere between a sneeze, a hiccough, and a baby's rattle – which she finally made out as

"Ha – "
     " – ha – "
          " – he – "
               " – he – "
                    " – ho – "
                         "– ho."

Alice thought she had never heard such mirthless laughter in all her life; and, hurriedly changing the subject, she began to say, "I find the weather awfully – ", when she was interrupted by Ping.

"No, no – leave off," it protested in a doleful voice. "My poor ribs are aching still."

"My dear, you ought to be on the stage, that you ought," said Pang, no less gravely.

"Why, the tears are streaming down my whiskers!" said Ping again. And, indeed, its large eyes *had* filled with tears – though, had she not known otherwise, Alice would have supposed them to be the result of some infinitely great sorrow. "But you must be impatient – " it went on.

" – to hear us cry."

"We-ll," said Alice hesitantly, "if you don't mind, I'd just as soon not – " Then she saw how dreadfully crestfallen they were: so she went on, " – put you to any trouble, that is."

"Bless you, child, but it's no trouble at all," said Ping, quite cheered up by the prospect.

Whereupon, Pang turned to it and said approvingly, "You took the very words out of my mouth!"

Alice hoped they were not going to ask her now to recount a *sad* story, as the saddest one she knew – about the little Princes in the Tower – made her sniffle only to think of it, which is just what started to happen to her.

"Not so fast, there!" said Ping.

"Have the courtesy to wait till our tale is told," said Pang.

So, deciding there was nothing else for it but to listen, Alice made herself as comfortable as she could on the beach, with her knees drawn up under her chin and her hands clasped over her legs.

In a solemn voice, Ping said, "This tale (by yours – "
" – truly) – " said Pang, ending the modest bow
begun by Ping (and I'm afraid I ca'n't tell you how it
managed to *complete* a bow without having first *started* it,
for I don't understand it at all).

" – I have named '*The Sands of Dee*' – " said Ping.

"Why, that's a coincidence," said Alice, "for I do
believe there's a poem – "

" – *and* its heroine – " said Pang loudly: " – its heroine
I have named – er, I have – "

"What is *your* name, my dear?" Ping unexpectedly
addressed Alice.

She told them.

"Now *there*'s your coincidence!" Pang exclaimed.

"The very name!"

Then, after a brief pause, they began – one line in
turn, as usual – to recite:

> " '*O Alice, call the hippopotami,*
>   *The hippopotami,*
>   *The hippopotami*
>   *Across the sands of Dee.*'
> *The maiden trembled. 'What a lot am I*
>   *Entrusted with!' said she.*

Her hippo-bell soon tinkled o'er the sand,
  Its tinkle crossed the sand,
  Its jingle swept the sand,
And echoed out to sea.
The thundering herd came down from off the land,
And flattened out was she."

While they recited these verses, sobbing so violently
that their tail began to whirl around – ("just like a
skipping-rope," thought Alice) – the two Cats would
peer closely into her face, putting her out altogether,
and from time to time one of them would break off to
inquire, "No tears yet, child?"

Though Alice tried and tried, she found that tears
simply *would not* come: and, since she did not like to
hurt their feelings, she decided to think very hard about
the little Princes again, so that when they began the
third stanza, her eyes had become quite misty:

"But still the boatmen hear a plaintive sigh,
  A sad, regretful sigh,
  A sad, remorseful sigh
  Which echoes out to sea:
'Why did I call the hippopotami
  Across the sands of – of – the sands of – ' "

"Well – *well!*" said Ping (for it was Pang that had spoken last), and it tapped a forepaw against a pebble. "What's the matter, pray?"

"I'm afraid – " Pang faltered, looking *very* unhappy, " – I'm afraid I may just have – " Its voice trailed off into silence.

"*Forgotten it?*" Ping screamed so shrilly that Alice jumped. "Not forgotten the last word *again?*"

"Well – not what you'd call *forgotten*, exactly," the wretched Pang tried to explain. "For example, I'm *pretty* certain it begins with one of the letters of the alphabet – that ought to narrow it down considerably."

"Idiot!" snapped Ping, giving the pebble such a furious kick along the beach, that it caused the sand to fly in all directions.

"Might I be of help?" Alice ventured to say. "It's the first time I've ever heard your tale, of course, but it does seem to me likely to be 'Dee'."

Pang turned to her excitedly. "What – you believe the word begins with a D, do you? Very like, very like. But let me think – how many words do I know beginning with a D? 'Dromedary'? 'The sands of Dromedary' – no, that wasn't it. 'Doctrine'? 'The sands of Doctrine' – no again! How about 'Dinner-service', one of my *very*

favourite words? 'The sands of Dinner-service'?" As if
to savour its rhythm, it repeated the phrase once or
twice over. "It has a nice familiar ring to it, wouldn't
you agree? And just the right length, too."

"You don't understand," said Alice. "What I really
meant was – "

"A duel!" Ping suddenly cried out.

"A duel?" said Alice, whose first thought was that it
was offering another suggestion.

"Why, naturally," said Ping: "Since *that* – " (pointing a scornful paw at Pang) " – never can remember the
last word, our tale always ends with a duel, you know.
To the death!"

"Have you fought many duels together?" Alice
asked.

"Oh, a dozen or so, at least," said Ping airily.

"If that's true, they can scarcely have been to the
death," Alice pointed out, "as you are both still here."

"What nonsense you talk, child!" said Ping. "Even
human beings must know a Cat has *nine* lives – so we
have eighteen between us."

Alice watched the two Cats take up their positions
back-to-back, with their tail curling up in the middle
like a huge question-mark, and two very rusty old

pistols clutched in their paws. ("And where did *they* come from?" she wondered. "I'm positive I'd have noticed them before.")

"The rules are these," said Ping in a business-like manner: "we take twenty paces each, then turn and fire. I trust you are able to count up to twenty?"

"To be sure I am," Alice replied a little sharply. "I think if I tried, I could count to a thousand!"

"A *thousand* paces – what a *much* more sensible idea!" cried Pang, waving its pistol about so carelessly that it started to make Alice nervous. ("I've often been told it's rude to point," she said to herself, "and I believe it's even ruder if one has a pistol in one's hand.")

But Ping only gave a derisive snort and ordered Alice to begin counting.

Though she felt she ought to urge them against fighting, Alice was simply too curious to know how Siamese-Twin Cats, attached at the tail, could possibly manage to march twenty paces away from each other. So she solemnly counted "One – two – three – four – ": and as their tail gradually straightened out, then stiffened all over, she became more curious than ever. Moreover, the sky was getting darker and darker, heavy clouds were casting fantastic shadows over the beach, and a storm looked about to burst at any minute.

As it happened, there *was* a loud thunder-clap a moment later – "more like a *bark*, really," thought Alice, who was so startled that she stopped counting – and she was almost struck on the head by a kitten that seemed to have dropped out of the heavens themselves. As all of its kind are able to do, it landed neatly on its feet; and, though a little shaken at first, it scampered away before Alice had got her breath back. No sooner had it done so, however, than another fell nearby, then another, then a third. Half astonished and half frightened, Alice saw that kittens – and, oh, there were a few darling puppies, too, among them – were beginning to fall in droves all around her.

Meanwhile, their quarrel forgotten, Ping and Pang had taken shelter inside a small and very dark cave.

"Step lively, you foolish creature – " Ping called out.

And Pang added impatiently, " – don't you know better than to stop out in the rain?"

"The *rain?*" said Alice, puzzled.

"Oh – it may only be raining kittens and puppies *now* – " said Ping.

" – but they'll turn to cats and dogs soon enough – " said Pang.

" – you mark my words!" said Ping again. (For, now the duel had been postponed, you see, they had returned to their former style of speaking.)

Quickly joining them under shelter – where it was all "Look out, now!" and "It's *your* fault – this is *my* half of the cave, you know!" and "Well, *you* almost took my eye out!" – Alice thought she had never witnessed anything so strange in her life. Hundreds of cats and dogs (and, as Pang had predicted, they *were* now fully grown, of every size, colour and breed) were pouring down as far as she could see. Once they had landed, they would all make a rush for lower ground, gathering there in huddles – "or *puddles*, I suppose one ought to say" – and the dogs would chase after the cats in ever-diminishing circles till, in a spray of sand, they disappeared altogether.

*   *   *   *   *

  *   *   *   *

*   *   *   *   *

  The storm abated as abruptly as it had begun, and the only trace it left was an untidy collection of footprints criss-crossing each other on the sand.

  "Now we really have to be going – " said Ping, holding out a paw to test whether the rain had stopped.

  " – mustn't be late for the election, you know," added Pang, and they started to run off along the beach.

  Alice, who had never seen an election before, felt sure it was something that would interest her greatly, so she called after them, "Who will be voting, if you please?"

  "Why, everybody . . . " a faint voice came back, though, as they were now almost out of earshot, she couldn't tell whether it belonged to Ping or Pang. Deciding, however, that if *everybody* was going to vote, *she* ought to as well, she hurried after them as fast as her legs would carry her.

CHAPTER III

"AND NINTHLY . . ."

Though the Siamese-Twin Cats were now only two small points on the horizon, Alice continued to run along the shore, which, far from being deserted, was getting quite crowded with animals and birds of every description. She had never known such an assortment of creatures except in picture-books or at the Zoo, "but in picture-books," as she said, "they're usually given one picture each to themselves, and in the Zoo they're kept behind bars." The thought of being trampled underfoot made her feel a little nervous, and remembering the poem which Ping and Pang had just recited to her, she particularly decided to stay clear of any hippopotami.

Alice's nearest neighbours were an auk, a barn-owl, a camel, and a dromedary. Not that she would have been able to identify either of the first two, however; and as for the last two, she found herself rather uncertain as to which was which. "A camel has two humps, I know – or is that a dromedary? How confusing it is," she sighed, and she began to repeat a lesson she had learnt in the schoolroom: " 'The Camel is the ship of the desert and has two funnels.' No, no, I mean – Dear me, everything seems to be coming out wrong. Anyway, it most likely *is* a camel," she concluded, "which arrived here the same way I did. For I'm sure I've read somewhere that a camel can pass through the eye of a needle."

On she sped. Overhead there buzzed a swarm of spelling bees: the birds, on the other hand, were all scurrying across the sand, causing Alice to remark – not for the first time, either – that, for creatures which *do* after all possess wings, birds seem to be tremendously fond of walking. "Now if *I* had wings," she said to herself, "I should think I'd want to fly everywhere – even on quite short errands. 'Please excuse me,' I'd say, 'but I just must flutter over to the haberdasher's for a fitting!' " And day-dreaming thus, Alice tore along, hoping that by following the crowd of animals, she would eventually arrive at the election.

Everything had been happening so queerly that she was not *too* surprised to see, out of the corner of her eye, an Elephant raised up on its hind legs on a little grassy knoll which formed the crest of the beach. At first, she thought it must be dancing, so wildly did it shake, but she soon realised that something had terrified it, though from where she was standing (she had stopped running, you see, and was very glad indeed of the rest) she could not see what. So she began to move forward stealthily, only to discover the Country Mouse reclining on a makeshift bed of reeds and grinning at the effect it was having on the poor Elephant. Alice, who could not bear to see any creature tremble so (even one so much larger than herself), considered shouting in the Country Mouse's ear in order to frighten it off but decided, after their earlier conversation, that that would be unnecessary: and she only whispered "Boo!" very softly.

The result was just as if she *had* shouted, though, for the startled Mouse leapt several inches clear into the air, crying out in a squeaky voice, " 'Eaven save us! It's that there 'Alley's Comet come again! It's all h'exploding now!" – whereupon it vanished in a cloud of sand.

The Elephant, meanwhile, produced a handkerchief from its trunk – ("just the way I keep my handkerchief inside my sleeve," thought Alice) – and set about laboriously mopping its brow. It was, Alice noticed, a very beautiful silk handkerchief with a fine curlicued E in one corner. The Elephant had not quite left off trembling, and after reassuring itself that the Country Mouse was out of sight, it sniffled fretfully in the direction in which it had fled, "Next time, take on somebody your own size, you – you great little bully, you!"

Alice didn't know whether she ought to comfort it or scold it. So she said, in her gentlest voice, "Shame on you – for a creature your size to be afraid of a mouse!"

The Elephant shamefacedly looked down its trunk at her. "I suppose *you* aren't afraid of insects, then?" was all it asked.

"Insects?" Alice repeated in a wondering tone. "Why, yes – I *don't* care much for insects. But a mouse is not an insect, you know."

"That all depends on the size *you* are," the Elephant pointed out, and proceeded to blow its trunk with its handkerchief (which sounded exactly the same as you blowing your nose, only much, much louder). At the same moment, a stray spelling bee brushed against Alice's face, causing her to shrink back in fright.

"There!" said the Elephant, which was beginning to recover its spirits.

Alice, however, though she had listened quietly enough to a lot of nonsense already, surprised herself by attempting to argue the point. "But even if a mouse *appears* as tiny to you as a bee does to me," she said thoughtfully, "it still ca'n't be an *insect*, you see, because it's a species – "

" – argument!" the Elephant bellowed, tucking the monogrammed handkerchief back inside its trunk with a flourish. "Indeed, it's a *very* specious argument! Therefore let's waste no more time upon it. Especially as – " It was interrupted by a distant cry of "The election's beginning!"

"Tusk, tusk!" said the Elephant crossly (or rather, that is what Alice imagined it said). "We're going to be late for the speeches. Come on!" And, without waiting for Alice's consent, it wrapped its trunk round her, lifted her up off the ground, and placed her squarely astride its back. A little uneasy at finding herself perched so precariously, she seized the Elephant's huge, flapping ears, one to each hand, as if they were the handle-pieces of a penny-farthing bicycle – ("At this height," she said to herself, "it ought to be tuppence-ha'penny, at least!") – and off they went.

Though she was out of breath with the speed at which it had all happened, Alice managed to pant, "Where is the election to be held?"

The Elephant replied, "In Hide-and-Seek Park, of course!", and began to run so remarkably fast that any further conversation was impossible.

*　　　*　　　*　　　*　　　*

　　*　　　*　　　*　　　*

*　　　*　　　*　　　*　　　*

The Elephant, with Alice on its back, had been racing forward at such a speed that during the last stretch the scenery became hardly more than a blur. When it came to a halt at last, then, and so abruptly that if Alice had not been grasping its ears, she would doubtless have tumbled head first down its trunk, she was not at all surprised to find that they'd left the beach behind. They were in a spacious green park, with sparkling fountains and shady paths and a wonderfully cool-looking river which curved between its lawns like a large silvery serpent slithering through the grass.

"So this is Hide-and-Seek Park," said Alice to herself. "I wonder if we are actually to play at Hide-and-Seek. I shouldn't think it was very suitable: anywhere would be awkward for an *elephant* to hide, but there are such wide open spaces here it'd be next to impossible." In any case, Alice hoped they would not, it having never been a favourite game of hers. "For when I'm It," she would confess, "it's just as though I *had* lost something, and that's not an awfully amusing thing to play at – and when I'm in hiding, it's strange, but I don't exactly want to be found out, of course, and yet I *do* want to be found out eventually, so that in the end I don't know what I want at all. Much nicer to go on a picnic."

But there seemed to be no chance of that, as the Elephant lumbered over to a corner of the park in which most of the birds and beasts were already assembled. They were all settling down in a half circle, and a deal of waddling and squawking and ruffling of offended feathers was undergone before everybody had made a satisfactory place for itself. Because of its size, the Elephant was obliged to remain at the rear, but Alice made her way through the crowd as courteously as she could – taking care not to tread on any of the smaller birds – in order to discover what it was they had gathered to see or hear.

Facing the assembly was a yellow-feathered, stout-bodied bird on a soap-box, clutching a rolled-up scroll of parchment in one claw and tapping the other with impatience on the edge of the box. Alice looked hard at the bird (which she guessed to be the Speaker), hoping to make out to which species it belonged: and as she looked, and looked ever harder and longer, she exclaimed, "Why, I do believe it's an Emu!", though she had never come across such a bird before. (Study the picture on this page if you want to understand better how she knew.)

"*It's got 'Emu' written all over it!*" somebody or something unexpected piped up near her.

Though Alice could not have explained why, she somehow knew that this had been spoken in Italics, for it had a queer emphasis to it, and there was something sloping and not quite straight-up-and-down about the pronunciation (and I hope you understand what I mean, for I'm sure *I* don't). Since she had been half conscious, above the general babble, of two voices raised nearby, mixed with a curious snapping noise, she turned round to see where they were coming from.

Immediately behind her was an elderly whale-like creature, clad in a dusty black professor's gown and mortar-board, holding a cane under one of its flappers and a large red Morocco-bound album under the other. The tassel of its mortar-board was being trimmed by an individual whom Alice recognised as an Italian Hair-dresser. ("Then it must have been he who spoke in Italics," she said to herself.) He stood only slightly more than half as tall as his client, and he had a white powdered face, wavy black hair, and a splendid waxed moustache. Alice was more alarmed to note that, instead of using a pair of scissors, the Hairdresser was snipping at the tassel with a small, scaly crocodile;

instead of a comb he had a caterpillar; and unconcernedly slung over his shoulder was an electric eel, "which I suppose he uses as a strop to sharpen his razors on," she thought, forgetting for the moment how absurd the whole notion was.

"I beg your pardon," she politely addressed the Hairdresser. "Did you speak?"

It was the whale that replied. "Never mind that," it said, carelessly brushing the crocodile away. "He ca'n't understand you, anyway, unless I translate the question into Italics, which would take much too long to do."

"I've never seen a whale, that wore a professor's gown," said Alice, looking at it with interest.

"It's because of my position, you know," was the reply: "Assistant Headmaster in the School of Whales. Really, though, I am a Grampus, which is to say, a ferocious man-eater," it went on; and though it had a kindly smile on its face as it spoke, Alice drew back in fright. "I said 'man-eater', child! I would never, never eat a little girl – we Grampuses are extremely particular about that sort of thing. Besides which, I wish you to hear the point I intend to make to the Emu. It's in verse, you'll be glad to know, and it's called 'For Want of a Nail'. Perhaps you're familiar with it?"

"Yes, I am," said Alice firmly: "so there's really no need – "

But nothing would stop the Grampus. And so it began:

"*For want of a nail –* " . . . ah, hm . . . " *– the kingdom was lost.*"

After a pause, it asked Alice, in a tone of profound self-satisfaction, "Well, my dear, what do you make of that? Of course, there *is* a part in the middle which I omitted – " ("Yes, one can say that you did," thought Alice) " – but that's the *gist* of it, you know. And it's my opinion the Emu is going to find it a difficult one to answer."

Alice was of the Grampus's opinion, though for a different reason, but she only asked, "What is the election for, if you please?"

"Heavens, I haven't the faintest notion," the Grampus replied with a feeble smile, as it turned to face the Emu.

There was a hush, while the Emu solemnly unrolled its scroll. Then, adjusting an enormous pince-nez over its beak (so enormous, in fact, that both its eyes would peer first through one glass, then through the other), it noisily cleared its throat as a signal for quiet: "Ahem!"

"Hear, hear!" a voice instantly cried from the audience. To Alice's surprise, it turned out to belong to the Crocodile.

The Emu glared at the Crocodile through each of the glasses of its pince-nez in turn, then proceeded, "Friends, Rom – "

"Hear, hear!" the Crocodile cried once more.

"Should it keep on interrupting so," Alice whispered to the Grampus, "no one *will* hear."

"Oh, but if there's anything it enjoys better than trimming tassels," it replied, fondly contemplating the offender, "it's hear, hearing a good speech."

The Emu tried to continue. "If I may be so – "

"Hear, hear!" the Crocodile interrupted yet again.

This time, it was too much for the Emu, and it angrily and *very* sharply said to the Hairdresser, "Another word from your crocodile, and I'll have it made into a travel-ling-bag!"

"I'm afraid, your – your – " the Grampus started to reply, " – your Emu-nence, I'm afraid he speaks nothing but Italics. However, I should be only too pleased to translate your kind observation, for I myself speak Italics, don't you know, though my command of it has got a little rusty of late, alas, and I fear that your

Emu-nence – I mean, your eloquence – must suffer in the translating thereof, nevertheless – "

"Oh, do get on with it, will you!" the Emu snapped back.

The Grampus seemed about to offer some gracious apology, but thought the better of it, and proceeded to translate the Emu's remark to the Hairdresser. (In Italics, as you would expect, it came out as *"Another word from your crocodile, and I'll have it made into a travelling-bag!"*)

Since the Hairdresser could hardly go paler than he

already was, he turned crimson instead. Then, with many embarrassed bows in the Emu's direction, he hastily removed the eel from off his shoulder and wrapped it round the Crocodile's jaws, tying it into a tight knot with an elaborate bow on top. "So that's what the eel was for," thought Alice: "and not for sharpening razors on. Well, well, I'd never have guessed it on my own."

The Emu began its speech at last. Alice, however, couldn't help feeling – though the Crocodile's interruptions had certainly been tiresome – that the remedy adopted was rather too violent. "It's the poor little eel I feel sorry for," she said to herself, "for, after all, *it* didn't make a nuisance of itself, and it ca'n't be very pleasant to be knotted up so. I'd like to be of comfort to it if I could, but that knot has been tied so tightly and goes off in so many different directions and then curls back on itself, that it's hard to know which end is which. Here's its little head, I'm sure," thought she, taking one of the loose ends in her hand and gently holding it up to study it more closely. "Why, no, it isn't – at least, I ca'n't seem to find either eyes or mouth, so they must belong to the *other* end. But that's wound up in such a tight ball, I'll never be able to unravel it. Poor thing, what dreadful cramps it must be having!"

While she was searching for some way to undo the knot ever so slightly, a single large tear started to roll down the Crocodile's scales. And, reassured by knowing its jaws were firmly shut, she began to caress it, saying the while "There, there" in a soft voice; but she stopped quickly enough when the Emu fixed on her with one of its glares, as if to say, "Don't *you* start there, there-ing now!"

"You needn't bother to console it," the Grampus whispered in her ear, "as crocodiles only weep crocodile tears, you know." And though she had never thought of it before in that light, it seemed to make sense, and she left off to attend to the speech.

"What an extremely fast talker the Emu must be!" thought Alice, for when she settled down to concentrate, it was already saying, "And *ninthly* – " "I wonder," she said to herself, "what the first eight points were." But, no matter how hard she tried, she could not pick up its train of thought at all. It was nothing but Definitions, Axioms, and Postulates, or else Uniform Rotation and Graduated Scansion, and mention was made several times of something called Rotten Burrows, which caused a great stir among the rabbits;

indeed, the only thing she was able to grasp was the fact that, when it addressed the assembled creatures as "My friends!", half of them would keenly sit up and pay attention while the other half, to her amusement, would chatter among themselves or play at tiddle-a-wink; but when its tone changed dramatically, and it addressed them as "Sufferers!", the order was reversed, and it was the former 'friends' which no longer cared to listen. "From which one can gather," Alice said to herself thoughtfully, "that if you don't happen to be a friend of the Emu, you are likely to come out all the worse for it."

While she was still trying to puzzle out a tenth of what the Emu had been saying, however, it brought its speech to an end by roaring out, "And *that*'s why I ask you all to vote for me!", so loudly that the feathers of the birds in the very front row began to flutter as though a little breeze had gone through them – those creatures which had nodded woke up with a start – and a Spotted Grebe protested to Alice, in an outraged tone, "How *dare* you accuse me of falling asleep! Why, I never so much as closed an eyelid!", though poor Alice had not uttered a word.

The Emu had meanwhile rolled up its parchment

scroll, and now inquired if there were any questions. At this the assembly became all of a sudden deathly quiet, and some of the birds shyly tucked their heads under their wings. Alice remembered that the Grampus wished to speak a few words, so she turned round to give it a meaningful look; when that had no effect, she nudged it just as gently as she could.

"Aarumph!" (or something like it) it grunted noisily, making Alice suspect that it, too, had fallen asleep. And then, aware that everybody was looking at it expectantly, it shut its eyes and stood for the longest time with one flapper pressed upon its forehead, as if deep in reflection, before asking at last, "When was the Battle of Hastings? Answer me that – *if* you can."

It wasn't at all the question Alice thought the Grampus would ask; and she half hoped the Emu would be unable to answer it, as History was her best school-subject, and she didn't mind in the least displaying her knowledge of it. But the Emu confidently replied "1066", for which it received a little round of applause.

"Pooh!" said the Grampus. "There's no such time of day."

"Oh, all right," sighed the Emu: "6 minutes past 11, if you prefer. It was due to begin at 11 o'clock sharp, you know, except that King Harold, better known as Harold the Unready, was not – well, he wasn't quite ready. Next question!"

Though Alice didn't know exactly how an election ought to be conducted, she was convinced that the Grampus's question had *very* little bearing on the matter, and she determined that she would pose a more searching one herself. "What promises do you make?" she called out (for she recalled hearing grown-ups talk about election promises).

The Emu gave her such a piercing stare, that any other little girl of her age would have been quite put out by it. "Ahem – what promises do I make? Why, I promise – I promise – I promise *not* to break my promise – and that's a promise! Next question!"

Alice wasn't entirely satisfied with this answer (in truth, she did not understand what it meant), and she continued, "But what do you stand for?"

"I stand for everything beginning with an F," the Emu replied in a rather aggressive tone, as if daring her to contradict it.

"Why?" asked Alice, puzzled, as she found such an attitude more curious than anything she had yet heard.

"No, *F*, I tell you!" repeated the Emu. "It's the Gnu

that stands for everything beginning with a Y."

When Alice started to turn the notion over in her mind, she came to the conclusion that it might be just as sensible as any other. "After all," she said to herself, "lots of good things begin with an F. There's freedom, for example, and facts and fair-play and fairyland and faith and families and Father Christmas and the fat of the land and festivities and foreign affairs and forgiving-and-forgetting and fruit-cake and fun. Of course," she added, slightly troubled, "so do falsehood and famine and fever and fear and foolishness and fiddle-faddle. I wonder which of the two kinds it stands for."

"Let me put your mind at rest," said the Emu, almost as though it had been able to read her thoughts. "I have just the poem for the occasion."

And it began:

> "If all the a's were capitals,
>   And small each w;
> If I forgot each i to dot,
>   whAt mischief would ensue!
>
> If I linked o's together,
>   And dropped the period;
> If lazily I crossed no t,
>   It might look very odd

If upside-down were h's,
    And halved each pair of e's;
If apostrophes were lost trophies,
    wчod ever fel Aι eAse?

And if, instead of just a j,
    I used its full name: jaybird;
And each u grew, and grew, and grew,
    Tчe jAybιrdoke mιgчι well sem lAboUred

Oh, f's the only letter
    The world can count upon;
For, without f's, there'd be no ifs,
    And dreams would end anon."

"Thank you," said Alice politely, though feeling more puzzled than ever. "It was a most interesting poem to listen to."

"I trust it cleared up all your little difficulties," the Emu said, with a complacent smile.

"*Almost* all," replied Alice unhappily. "I feel certain it *does* have a meaning somewhere, and I almost understand it already. Perhaps it would be easier for me to follow if I had it written down."

"Perhaps it would," said the Emu, "and then again perhaps it wouldn't. Since I don't intend to write it down, we'll never know."

"Was Anon the name of its author?" Alice went on,

for she had sometimes learnt Anon's poems at school.

The Emu drew itself up to its full height and puffed out its chest. "*I* am the sole author, Miss!" it said in an offended tone.

This caused quite a squabble, as the Country Mouse insisted *it* had written the poem – its num-de-plum (as it called it, rhyming it with 'tum-ti-tum') was Anon, which, as was as clear as the beak on the Emu's face, was short for Anonymouse – in fact, it had written *all* the poems signed Anon in the anthologies – and it would *very much* like to see somebody prove the contrary! However, as the Mouse had also claimed to have written the Complete Works of Shakespeare, nobody paid any attention to it.

For the moment had come for the counting of votes, which, there being only one candidate, Alice reckoned should not take very long. The Emu produced a little gavel and gong, and loudly asked, "Who will open the bidding?"

It was a dabchick which answered first, followed quickly by a hedgehog, then by a stork, and soon all the creatures were making bids, each one higher than the last. "Why, this is not an election at all," Alice said to the Grampus: "it's really what they call an *auction*."

"Much the same thing, my dear," the Grampus airily replied, and it shrugged where its shoulders would have been if it had had any shoulders.

In the end, only Alice had not voted, and noticing the Emu glaring at her again, she hastily cast her vote along with the rest. The Emu raised its gavel and said in a solemn voice, "Going . . . going . . . gong!" – then, blushing, it corrected itself, " – that's to say, Going . . . going . . . *gone!*" And as it struck the gong, to Alice's astonishment everybody vanished at once and she found herself alone in the park.

CHAPTER IV

AUTO-BIOGRAPHY OF A GRAMPUS

But Alice was *not* alone – or rather, not completely alone. For she soon spied the Grampus and the Italian Hairdresser a little way off, strolling towards her. As she watched them, the Grampus opened the album it was carrying and made a mark in it with a thick pencil which, from the number of times it was obliged to lick the lead point, she imagined must be very blunt indeed. At the same time, the Hairdresser was busily brushing loose threads off the Grampus's gown with what looked like a small but extremely hairy puppy: for every thread it removed, Alice could not help noticing that the puppy left at least a dozen hairs of its own, so that the gown ended up far less tidy than when it had begun.

The Grampus approached Alice and greeted her affectionately. "Ah, there you are, my dear! Your name is Boris, is it not?"

"Why, no," replied Alice, who was rather taken aback by the question: "it's Alice, if you please."

The poor Grampus looked quite crestfallen; anxiously poring over its album, it muttered to itself, "Not Boris, not Boris! Really, I ca'n't conceive how such a mistake could have occurred!" It addressed Alice again. "Are you *sure* your name isn't Boris? Think, child, it's most important. It could be, for instance, that you haven't got a good memory for names?"

"I have a *very* good memory for names," said Alice; and though feeling a little foolish, she added, "especially for my own!"

"Hm, yes, I take your point," said the Grampus thoughtfully, as, with downcast eyes, it looked long at the album, making Alice even more curious to know what it contained, for all she could see was a large capital I on the cover. Then suddenly brightening up, it began to repeat over and over, "Boris – Alice. Alice – Boris. Oh, how silly of me!" it exclaimed at last, blinking at the open page. "I believe it *does* say 'Alice', after all! See, child, if I am not right!"

The Grampus held out the album for Alice's inspection. It was scribbled over from top to bottom, and even into the margins, but she was able to make out, quite clearly, the entry: I SHALL MEET A FEMALE CHILD NAMED BORIS. It was Alice's opinion that the name was certainly 'Boris'; but not wishing to hurt the Grampus's feelings (it was hovering over her with an expectant gleam in its eye), and thinking it most unlikely it could *ever* meet a female child named Boris, she said, in a deliberate voice, "Ye-es, if you look at it from an angle – *and* you half shut your eyes – *and* you hold it about a foot away – why, there would seem to be no doubt of it. The name is 'Alice'."

"How glad I am to hear you say so!" exclaimed the Grampus, visibly relieved. "I really shouldn't have liked to quarrel with you so soon after we've met." It drew the blunt pencil from out the album's spine, licked it two or three times, and inscribed this mark: opposite the entry in question.

"I don't wish to pry," said Alice politely, "but I'm afraid I don't understand what sort of book it is."

"It's my Auto-biography," replied the Grampus simply.

Alice had to think for a minute or two, for she did not

know what an Auto-biography was, and so gave the Grampus an opportunity to explain. "You see, child, I am a *very* absent-minded Grampus – "

"Just like Great-Uncle Henry!" Alice cried out, forgetting for her part that it's not considered polite to interrupt one's elders. "I mean, he isn't a Grampus, you know," she added, in case there might be any confusion, "but – " (and now she cleverly imitated her Great-Aunt) " ' – the number of times he has left home *with* an umbrella and returned home *without* it, you would not believe!' "

"Goodness, that's nothing at all," replied the Grampus, with a melancholy smile. "*I* am so absent-minded, I often go out *without* an umbrella and return *with* one! *I* am so absent-minded," it went on, warming to its theme, "I sometimes forget I *am* absent-minded, and remember everything!"

"Then I suppose the first thing you remember is your own absent-mindedness?" Alice asked.

"Exactly so," replied the Grampus: "which means that I forget everything all over again! But what was I saying?"

"That you were a very absent-minded Grampus – "

"So much so, indeed, that I decided – oh, many,

many years ago – to write the story of my life, in advance, so that I could live it out afterwards. This way, I am sure to remember. Of course," it added, with a shade of vexation in its voice, "it's not always easy to make everything work out, and it'll sometimes happen that I fall a little behind in my timetable." Here it frowned at the Hairdresser, who was fussily combing out the tassel of its mortar-board with his caterpillar. "*Be off with you!*" the Grampus shouted at him in Italics. "*You've made me late enough as it is!*"

The Hairdresser stuffed the caterpillar inside the breast pocket of his coat and began slowly to withdraw, bowing so low that Alice almost expected his nose to touch the ground.

The Grampus wriggled uncomfortably for a few moments, a stray thread from the tassel having got lodged under its gown, then it once more set to studying the open page of its Auto-biography. "Let me see," it said, sucking the tip of its pencil. "Ah, here we are – 'I SHALL GO HOME BY TRAIN, ACCOMPANIED BY THE SAID BORIS – ' (aarumph, I should say ALICE). Good, the train leaves in just three minutes."

"Why, then, oughtn't we to hurry?" said Alice, looking round her for some sign of a railway station.

"Not at all," replied the Grampus carelessly. "According to my Auto-biography, I shall – to my *great* distress – miss the first train, though we shall be in plenty of time for the following one. But do remind me, child, to be properly distressed. It's just the kind of detail I tend to forget."

Though it was all Alice could do to stifle a burst of laughter, she gravely said, "You may depend upon me. But why did you want to miss the train? For surely it'd have been easier and more convenient to catch it?"

The Grampus reflected on this for a moment. Then, to Alice's surprise, it asked, "Do you like to play at Snakes and Ladders?"

"Yes, quite a lot," she said. "But I ca'n't see – "

"You wouldn't find it very amusing to play Snakes and Ladders without any Snakes, I think," said the Grampus. "Well, life is just like Snakes and Ladders. After all, in life you will find Snakes – and, ha, there are Ladders too, aren't there?" it added, pleased that the comparison had worked out so well. "And the great thing in life is to know how to *climb* the Snakes."

"I wonder you aren't ever sorry to have written it all down beforehand," Alice remarked after a pause. "You see, the thing I love most in the world is surprises, and like this you wo'n't be able to have any."

"You're forgetting, my dear," replied the Grampus, "that I wrote my Auto-biography so many years ago – everything in it comes as a surprise. Not always a pleasant one either, I'm afraid. For instance, when I was looking it up just now to find out what I am to do next, I couldn't help taking a peek ahead – it's against the rules, but *very* hard to resist, you know – and I noticed that, once we arrive on the station platform, I am to be attacked by a bloodthirsty band of brigands and tied up across the rails. You, child, will save me from the oncoming train," it said calmly to Alice, as if with utter confidence in her ability to perform the rescue. "Now, when I wrote that down," it explained, a little doubt-fully, "I fancy I imagined it would be rather fun, don't you know. Now I'm a tiny bit less certain it will be." And, for a moment, the prospect made the Grampus look quite despondent.

But they finally arrived at a little country station, which, with its neatly tended window-boxes and flower-beds, its freshly swept platform, and its dark and cosy waiting-room, seemed to Alice a concentration of all the little country stations she had ever seen. There was also an oval ticket-window, and though its interior was enveloped in such gloom that it prevented Alice from discovering what kind of creature might be sitting behind it, so that at first she thought it was empty, she heard the Grampus ask for "*two* tickets for myself, if you please, and one for my young companion".

Alice felt sure that, if she were to pose the question about which she was aching with curiosity, she would be given an even more curious answer; but the temptation became too strong, and she said to the Grampus, as she took her ticket from it, "Thank you very much; but why do you buy *two* for yourself?"

"I always pay for two seats in the train," explained the Grampus, "because when I am travelling, I'm usually *beside myself* with anxiety, you know. So that it would be dishonest for me to purchase only one ticket."

Alice once more found it difficult to keep a straight face, as they stepped on to the platform. She did remember, however, to remind the Grampus of the distress it was to feel at having missed the earlier train.

"Why, thank you, my dear, I *had* forgotten, as you see," said it, smiling politely at her; then, after asking her if she would not mind looking to its album and cane for a few seconds, it suddenly allowed itself to be overcome by such pitiable distress that Alice was quite shocked by its haggard appearance. It began to wave its flappers back and forth in an agitated way, and pace up and down along the platform, groaning to nobody in particular (for there was nobody else on the platform but Alice, and the Grampus did not look once in her direction). "Oh, my sainted Bradshaw! Didn't I say that we'd miss the train? Didn't I? And would you listen? Not you! *You* knew better! 'What does Bradshaw know of it?' says you. 'We have lots of time,' says you. Lots of time, indeed! Now, all on your account, we have more time on our hands than a centipede makes footprints!" – whereupon its features just as abruptly softened.

"Nothing like a little vocal distress to get the blood circulating again!" said the Grampus cheerfully, making a fresh mark in the album. "You should try it some time. Now for the brigands," it went on, with a sigh. "Ah well, like as not it'll all be over in five minutes or so."

The problem was, that there were no brigands to be seen. The platform was empty, and remained empty; and though the Grampus peered into both the waiting-room and the station-master's office, and inquired at the ticket-window if, by any chance, a band of bloodthirsty brigands had lately bought tickets there, it seemed less and less likely as the time passed that they were going to appear at all.

"Where *can* they have got to?" mumbled the Grampus, looking round it every way.

"Perhaps the brigands have also written Auto-biographies," Alice ventured to suggest, "and in theirs it's written for them to miss the next train, just as we missed the last one." In fact, the more she thought of it, the better pleased Alice was with her theory, which struck her as quite the most sensible thing she had heard said all day.

But her companion merely stared at her – ("just as if *I* were the one who was mad," as Alice afterwards described it to her sister) – then proceeded to fan her head with its album, which was so heavy that, though it did not much refresh her, it soon made the Grampus quite hot and bothered to wave it about so.

"What *are* you talking about?" it shouted, rather rudely, in Alice's opinion. "Sit down, my dear child, and take the weight off your head! You must be feverish!" – and it all but pushed poor Alice on to the nearest bench on the platform.

Less than a minute later, however, it dragged her to her feet again. "I'm afraid there's nothing else for it: we shall have to do the thing ourselves. Fortunately, I brought a length of rope with me for just such an eventuality," it said, pulling the rope out from beneath the folds of its gown. "Actually," it whispered into her ear (even though the platform was still deserted), "I *always* carry it about me, don't you know. It comes in handy for tying a knot on my flapper whenever I wish to remember something."

With much huffing and puffing, the Grampus began to climb down on to the rails; and as it was rather elderly, and encumbered with its Auto-biography, Alice assisted it as well as she could, though once or twice, when it seemed about to slip and started to panic, she was almost struck on the face by its flappers.

"I never realised," gasped the Grampus, "that climbing down on to a railway line could be such uphill work!"

Alice then lowered herself down, taking care not to graze her knees – only to discover that they had left the rope behind, out of reach, on the platform. So she had to clamber back up again, propping herself on the Grampus's back, while it hurried her along with "Oh, do make haste, child! There's so little time to spare! I only hope the train decided not to take a short cut!"

"Do the trains hereabouts often take short cuts?" Alice asked, trying to picture how it might happen, as, with rope in hand, she climbed back down on to the rails.

"Only the first-class compartments," replied the Grampus: "the others must make the long way round."

But there was no time for further explanations, for the moment had come for Alice to tie the Grampus up. It proved a hardly less ticklish task than the business of climbing down in the first place, as the Grampus either *could* not, or *would* not, find a comfortable position on the railway line. For example, when it stretched out at a right angle to the rails, it complained of them digging sharply into its back; and when it lay full on, it would wriggle this way and that, and the folds of its gown would catch beneath the metal bars, so that Alice began to wonder whether they would ever succeed before the train came puffing into the station, "and it wouldn't be permitted to behave in such a childish manner, I know," she said to herself crossly, "if there were *real* brigands tying it up." Still, after a great deal of fidgeting, the Grampus appeared to have got settled at last, and Alice wound the rope about its waist, though not too tightly.

"Are you all right?" she anxiously inquired, keeping an eye on the little tunnel through which the train was due to arrive.

"Yes, thank you," the Grampus replied, with a strained smile: "comfortable enough, considering. And if you will just hand over my Auto-biography – "

"Your Auto-biography?" said Alice. "Is this the time – "

"Fiddlesticks!" said the Grampus in an impatient tone. "You've heard it said, I'm sure, that when one is in mortal danger, one's whole life passes before one's eyes. Naturally, with a memory like *mine*, it'll make much better sense if I just lie here perusing the pages of my Auto-biography."

And that is what the Grampus did, as Alice looked on, at what was the most extraordinary sight she could ever remember seeing. It was soon absorbed in the history of its life, and perhaps might have lain there quite happily for hours, had not a train whistle sounded in the distance.

"Sir? Mr. Grampus!" said Alice, not liking to interrupt its reading, but feeling strongly that she ought to, nevertheless. "I think I hear the train approaching."

"What's that?" The Grampus nervously started up.

"The train, you say? Why didn't you tell me before, you silly goose?"

"Because I only just this minute heard it," said Alice, a little sulkily.

"That's a poor excuse, I must say," remarked the Grampus. "If I weren't here to jog you along, I can see I'd *never* get rescued! Well, what are you waiting for now, child? Undo me, and don't be all day about it!"

"How rude the creatures are!" thought Alice. "Why, it would be no more than it deserved if I decided to leave it right there."

But she was much too kind-hearted to carry out her threat, and so everything was reversed. Alice began to unwind the rope, a task made no easier by its rapidly getting entangled with the Grampus's Auto-biography, which it was clutching to its breast as though its life depended upon it (which *was* true in a sense, of course). And when that part had been successfully performed, they climbed back on to the platform: Alice first, supported on the Grampus's back as before; then the Grampus, as, with further huffing and puffing, she hauled it up after her. This time it left its cane behind, lying across the railway line, so Alice had to climb back down and retrieve it. In fact, it was only a few seconds after they had both reached safety on the platform, with all the Grampus's belongings beside them, that a little train came steaming through the tunnel.

"Well," said the Grampus, smiling with condescension at Alice, "that went off quite satisfactorily, I think."

*　　　　*　　　　*　　　　*　　　　*

　　*　　　　*　　　　*　　　　*

*　　　　*　　　　*　　　　*　　　　*

"Truly," the Grampus went on, now settled in a compartment at a seat by the window, "the rescue was so much cosier, just the two of us, with nobody else to get in the way." It made a fresh mark in its album. "And since you acted so promptly, and only forgot to do things once or twice, I've decided to overlook the nonsense you spoke on the platform. Brigands writing their Auto-biographies, indeed! What an imagination you have, child!"

"I only meant – " Alice began to say.

"*Don't* mean!" the Grampus roared at her. "Think, speak, mention, assert, deliberate, declare – even opine, if you will – but never, never *mean*! Why, the world would be in a fine stew if just anybody felt free to mean, where and when they pleased!"

"I don't understand what you – " Alice was about to say "mean", but she managed to correct herself in time, and concluded, " – what you are saying."

"Meaning, my dear, is a rare and precious substance," the Grampus gravely replied: "so precious that, if my opinion were asked about it, it should be preserved under a bell jar in the Museum – on view to the Public, Tuesdays and Fridays, at sixpence a time."

"But dictionaries are full of meanings," objected Alice, who remembered consulting one not so long ago.

"Full of *meanings*, perhaps, but empty of *meaning*," said the Grampus. "As I ought to know, for I tried reading a dictionary once – just as a change from my Auto-biography, you understand – but the story in it was the dullest and most meaningless I ever read. And the reason for that is, that the best meanings ca'n't ever be written down, that's how precious they are."

"I think I should have to hear an example," Alice cautiously replied.

"And so you shall!" it exclaimed, and it suddenly began to recite the following:

> *"In spring the farmer sows his field:*
> *What crops in autumn will it yield?*
> *In spring the farmer's wife sews, too:*
> *A baby's mittens – pink or blue?*
> *From early morn, with cock a-crowing,*
> *They both set busily to – "*

The Grampus left off to address Alice. "And what do you think the next word ought to be?"

"I'm pretty well certain it's 'sewing'," replied Alice.

"Quite right. And how would you write it down, may I ask?"

Alice did not even bother to reflect before answering. "Why, that's easy: s-e-w-i-n – I mean – " she broke off thoughtfully, " – no, it ca'n't be that, for it would only apply to one kind of sewing. So it should be: s-o-w-i – " she broke off again. "Except that now it only applies to the *other* kind! I know – it should be spelt: s-..." More confused than ever, Alice fell silent for a moment. "Now I understand," she said, brightening up: "the word ca'n't be spelt at all, because – "

"*That*'s what I call a meaning!" the Grampus interrupted her in triumph. "And I trust you'll remember this lesson in years to come," it went on, looking severely at Alice, "for you've learnt more from me to-day than you'd learn at school in a month of Sundays!"

"That's true enough," Alice replied, "as I don't go to school on Sundays."

The Grampus chose to ignore this last remark. "As for brigands writing Auto-biographies," it continued, "that's *quite* impossible. An Auto-biography is written in the first person, which is 'I', and there ca'n't be more than one first person, now can there, or it'd be 'we', so let's have an end of such foolish chatter!"

It turned to its album again, opening it at the same page as before. "Oh – *Oh!*" it cried. "Now this is irksome, this is really most irksome!"

"Why, what's the matter?" Alice asked, with great curiosity.

"Oh, it really isn't good enough!" wailed the Grampus. "It's written here – " (jabbing the page with its flapper) " – *clearly* written here that our train is to be swept aloft by a hurricane. Well, and where is it, that's what I want to know! Where is it?"

Alice couldn't help thinking that, if the Grampus insisted upon having brigands and a hurricane all on a single train journey, it ought not to be surprised that so few of the entries in its Auto-biography ever came to pass; and though she didn't believe there was any real chance of a hurricane descending on the train, she gently suggested that "Perhaps it's all for the best, you know, that there is none. They're awfully dangerous things."

"HURRICANE is what I wrote," the Grampus replied, a little testily, "so hurricane there should be. Besides," it added in a careless tone, "*I* should be in no danger, since I'd be the 'i' of the hurricane, don't you see."

"But what about me?" asked Alice, though, as she couldn't at all follow the Grampus's logic, she hardly knew why she posed the question.

"You would be the 'u', of course. There's a 'u' in hurricane, too, in case you didn't know it. Oh, but what's the use in talking about it all, and making such plans together!" it said, wringing its flappers in despair.

"And what am I to do about this entry in my Auto-biography?"

Since the Grampus was looking *very* despondent, Alice racked her brains for a solution to its problem; and suddenly she found one.

"Look here," she explained, pointing at the sentence in the album: "see how widely spaced the words are. Why, I'd say there was quite enough room for you to introduce the word NOT between THE TRAIN WILL and BE SWEPT ALOFT BY A HURRICANE, so that nobody would ever know the difference."

The Grampus contemplated the page, squinting at it from every possible angle (including upside-down); then it broke into a smile of delight, and said, "What a *splendid* idea – and there's nothing in the rules against it!" And without a moment's hesitation, it drew out its pencil, licked the point vigorously, and inserted the extra word.

But nothing, thought Alice, could ever be cut-and-dried with such a creature. For, only a minute after studying the result with satisfaction, the Grampus glanced out of the compartment window, and what it saw there made it exclaim in a loud voice, "Gracious, we've passed the station where I must get off! Oh, you shouldn't, you know," it said to Alice reproachfully, "you really shouldn't."

"Shouldn't what?" Alice asked.

". . . Give me ideas beyond my station."

When Alice looked out of the window in her turn, however, the view seemed strangely familiar. So preoccupied had she been with the Grampus's problems, she had scarcely cast a glance at the passing scenery; and it was only now that she realised that the scenery had not been passing at all. "I'm positive that's the same little hill I saw when we entered the compartment," she said to herself, "and, now I come to think of it, I don't recall the train moving or lurching or doing any of the other things trains are supposed to do." And taking a closer look at her surroundings, she discovered that she was not in a train compartment at all, but in a dark little room with faded brown wall-paper, cobwebs on the ceiling (where the luggage racks had been before), and a writing-desk piled high with musty books and papers. There was also a pungent but not unpleasant smell, which, after a moment, Alice worked out as being composed of pipe tobacco, cough drops, blotting-paper and cinnamon, in roughly equal parts.

"Why, it's a study," she exclaimed: "what I think is

called a brown study. And now that I know what it looks like, the next time it's brought into the conversation, I shall be able to say I've been in one."

In the gloom Alice finally made out the figure of the Grampus – it was fast asleep, with its Auto-biography on its lap, in a deep leather armchair by the window. Though she coughed politely once or twice, she failed to rouse it; and so she tiptoed over to the door, opened it without making a sound, and stepped out into the sunshine. The little hill which she had seen from the window lay straight ahead.

CHAPTER V

JACK AND JILL

Nearing the hill, Alice saw that it was a very little one indeed – "not much more than a mound, really," she said to herself – and the first thing to do, she decided, would be to climb up to the top and inspect the surrounding countryside. What particularly intrigued her, however, was something she noticed on the top itself, and which looked, from where she was standing, remarkably like a well. "But what is a well doing up there?" thought Alice. "After all, a well's something you make by digging deep into the ground, so I should say a hill was a very unsuitable spot for it altogether, as you'd only have to dig the deeper!"

She might have pursued these reflections further,

had they not been interrupted by a great uproar coming from above her, one in which screams, loud cries for help, and a tinny clattering noise were all mixed up in confusion. And before Alice knew what was happening, somebody had rolled down the hill straight into her, knocking her off her feet and sending her sprawling. A moment afterwards, to the accompaniment of high-pitched squeals, somebody else fell on top of *them*; and there they all lay, in a complicated tangle of limbs.

Quite dazed by her tumble, Alice sat up and tried to collect her thoughts. Beside her, the two creatures who had collided with her lay stretched out on the grass, moaning and groaning in a fashion pitiable to hear. Her immediate impression of them was that they were both *extremely* thin – "just skin and bones, almost," she thought, "and not so much skin, at that." But when she peered more closely at them (which she was able to do, as they were still strenuously rubbing their heads, and had not yet paid the slightest attention to her), she realised that they were, in fact, nothing more than little stick figures, such as she remembered seeing in the pictures of her first reading-books. (So you must not suppose, when you look at the drawing on the next page, that our artist has become all of a sudden very lazy.) One was a boy, who had on a pair of short leather breeches and a merry little felt hat with a feather sticking up out of it: the other, a girl, wore a pretty pink dress with frills, half concealed by a clean white pinafore.

The boy sat bolt upright and stared into Alice's face: with not a word of greeting or introduction, he said, "Why don't you look where *I'm* going? Because of your carelessness I very nearly broke my crown!"

Alice swallowed down as well as she could her

annoyance at such bad manners, for the word 'crown' had made her ears tingle with excitement. "Perhaps he's a young Prince in disguise," she said to herself, for she had read tales of Caliphs strolling through the streets of Baghdad by moonlight in – "in *un*fancy dress, I imagine you would call it, since Royalty are in real fancy dress every day of the week. It's true," she went on thoughtfully, "that if he *were* in disguise, he'd not likely be wearing his crown." But that did not worry her as she began to search around in the grass.

"What *are* you doing?" said the boy, in a snappish tone.

"I thought I'd help you look for your crown," Alice replied politely. "It must have slipped off when you – " She interrupted herself, for she remembered the little felt hat, which was still on his head, though it was now a trifle askew: its feather had been quite flattened down and looked like a corkscrew which had been drawn through the wringer.

"Are you certain you were wearing your crown to-day, your Majesty?" she asked, looking pointedly at his hat.

"My crown, yes!" he replied impatiently. "My bean, my noodle, my head! Really," he added in a supercilious voice, turning to address the little girl, who was crossly trying to smooth some ugly creases out of her pinafore, and had taken no notice of their conversation, "I ca'n't think what children are taught these days!"

"Why, I don't believe you're any older than I am," said Alice with spirit, now she knew he was not a Prince.

"How old *are* you, when you are at home?"

"The same age as here," replied Alice (but she added inwardly 'I think', as, with everything that had been happening to her, she was no longer absolutely certain): "seven years and ten months."

"I am seven years, eleven months and six days exactly!" the boy exclaimed in triumph. "And in *my* day children were taught to be more respectful towards their elders."

Not wishing to enter into such an unpromising argument, Alice turned to the girl, who was still fussing over her pinafore.

"Perhaps you'd like me to help you?" she suggested good-naturedly.

"*You!*" replied the girl contemptuously. "Haven't *you* done enough harm already?" She tugged at her pinafore so violently, that Alice was afraid she was going to tear it in the end. "I've got it spick," she went on, gritting her teeth, "but I sha'n't be satisfied till it's span as well!"

Since, for the moment, neither of them seemed very disposed to be friendly, and the boy sat straightening the feather in his hat while the girl continued to give vicious little tugs at her pinafore, Alice began to treat her forehead, which had been quite badly bruised in the fall.

"The best cure for a headache, you know – " said the boy, pausing dramatically before speaking again, " – is to get rid of it! There – I offer you my services free of charge. Next time, it'll cost you *twice* as much."

Alice was on the point of remarking that she hoped there would not be a next time, when she noticed, some way off, a large metal pail; and she realised that it was that which had hurt her so. And suddenly recalling the very first poem she had ever learnt, she cried out, "Why, I know who you are! You're Jack and Jill!"

"And how do you come to know that, young lady?" the boy asked.

"Because of the nursery rhyme, of course!" Alice replied. "Let me recite it to you."

"Pah!" said Jill: "when you've heard one nursery

rhyme, you've heard them all!"

Alice proceeded nevertheless:

> *"Jack and Jill went up the hill*
> *To fetch a pail of water.*
> *Jack fell down and broke his crown,*
> *And Jill came tumbling after."*

"I call that a *very* childish poem!" said Jack with a toss of the head. "The rhymes are too stale – 'Jill', 'hill', 'down', 'crown' – and as for 'water' and 'after', why, they don't rhyme at all, as I can hear. The ending isn't so, besides. If it hadn't been for your clumsiness, I'd *never* have fallen down!"

Though Alice certainly could not agree with Jack's last remark, she decided that it might be more tactful to remain silent. Without even waiting a moment, however, there was Jill snorting provokingly, "Pah! When you've heard one silence, you've heard them all!"

"I was only a little girl, you see, when it was taught me," said Alice finally: "not much more than a baby. We had to learn it off by heart."

"When you say that, do you mean that you know it backwards?" Jack asked her.

"I should say I do."

"Then recite it so."

"I beg your pardon?" said Alice, puzzled by this request.

"*Backwards*, if you please," he repeated, more loudly.

"Oh, but you don't understand," Alice tried to explain. "I should have said – "

"That you should!" Jack shouted at her. "But since you didn't, proceed."

"You might set it to music, too, while you're about it," Jill added, in a bored voice.

So, hardly knowing what was expected of her, Alice opened her mouth, and, to her surprise, this is what she heard herself sing: (It was set to a tune which was a little like '*I dreamt I dwelt in marble halls*' – a little like '*Pop Goes the Weasel*' – and whenever it wasn't like either of these, it sounded just like '*God Save the Queen*'.)

> "*Back uphill rolled Jack and Jill*
> *Until Jack's crown was mended.*
> *They poured the pail down in the well,*
> *Then backwards redescended.*"

The moment the verse came to an end, Alice clasped both hands over her mouth, as it was very disturbing to have sounds, and not only sounds but real words and music, emerge from it of their own accord, "without my ever having put them there," she said to herself: "and hearing the story told backwards, it made me think that Time was somehow all squeezed up, as in a concertina."

"Yes indeed, it would go nicely on a concertina," said Jack, nodding as if he were agreeing with her thoughts, though he had quite misunderstood what she meant. "Talking of concertinas," he went on, "let's have it in French now."

"In French?" repeated Alice, somewhat dismayed. "But I only know so very little."

"It's only a very little poem," said Jack in an imperious tone. "Begin."

And Alice discovered, once again, that the words came without any bidding from her:

> *"Jacques et Jacqueline sont montés à la colline*
> *Pour remplir un gros seau de l'eau.*
> *Jacques est tombé en se cassant le nez,*
> *Jacqueline aussi – "*

"Grosso modo," said Jack sagely, completing the rhyme. (The phrase is Latin, you see, and it means 'more or less'.) "You were a trifle free with names, you know – " here Jill scowled more than usual at Alice " – but otherwise it'll do well enough. And don't worry if you ca'n't understand it. When you are as old as I am, you'll find that poetry is as simple a matter as 'How d'ye do'."

"It may surprise you," Alice replied – ("It does," said Jill) – "but I do know a few poems myself." She was not at all unhappy to have this opportunity of listing them, as she believed she knew more than most children of her age. "I know '*Twinkle, twinkle, little star*' and – "

"Pah!" said Jill: "when you've seen one star twinkle, you've seen them all!"

"Now, I've read somewhere that that isn't the case at all," Alice said thoughtfully to herself, though, because they were such touchy creatures, she didn't care to voice her opinion aloud, for fear of offending them again.

"What did I say!" screamed Jill. "Heard one, heard them all! This new silence of yours is exactly the same – word for word, I swear – as the last!"

"Why, that *isn't* so," Alice protested. "The words I spoke – I mean, that I *didn't* speak – during this silence were quite different from those of the silence before." But she couldn't help thinking to herself, "What nonsense we are talking!"

At this Jack suddenly got to his feet, and though he wobbled a little on his thin stick legs, he went over to the pail, lifted it up, and peered inside. "Just what I suspected," he said, and sadly shook his head: "because of *you* – " (looking hard at Alice) " – the water has spilled over. Which means we shall have to climb all the way back up the hill and fill it again."

"But what is the water for?" Alice inquired. "I've often wondered, you see, and the nursery rhyme makes no mention of it."

Whereupon Jack began to explain that it was for the . . . (but, though she listened as intently as she could, Alice was unable to make out whether what he said was 'eels' or 'L's') . . . which were to be fed to . . . (and again Alice couldn't be sure if the word she heard was 'whales' or 'Wales'). Thinking that she might better understand by seeing for herself, she stepped over beside him and looked down into the pail; and though most of the water had indeed spilled out on to the grass, she saw what, at first glance, certainly *looked* like a tangle of eels, except that they were the queerest eels you could ever imagine, as all their squirming about was done at strict ninety-degree angles, just like L's after all.

This was a puzzler for Alice. After a pause, she asked,

"Do whales – or Wales, I ought to say – eat L's – I mean, eels?" (As you can see, she was rather embarrassed that she didn't know the true pronunciation for each word.)

"Why, of course they do!" was Jack's reply. "And most of all in Llanfairpwllgwyngyllgogerychwyrndrob-wllllantysiliogogogoch," he added carelessly.

"I beg your pardon," said Alice, more puzzled than ever: "but would you mind repeating that – that word?"

"What a dull stick you are," said Jack impatiently, "and no mistake!" ('Stick' was a most unfortunate description for *him* to use, thought Alice.) Llanfairpwll-gwyngyllgogerychwyrndrobwllllantysiliogogogoch. Oh no, I mean: Llanfairpwllgwyngyllgogerychwyrn-drobwlll*l*antysiliogogogoch! – I dropped an 'l' the first time, as you no doubt noticed."

Alice's brain was in a whirl, but she was determined to learn as much as she could about this strange word, which was quite the longest she had ever heard.

"Excuse me," she began politely, "but where – what – is – " And there she left off, as she fancied she would never be able to say even the half of it. (Could you?)

"You mean Llanfairpwllgwyngyllgogerychwyrn-drobwllllantysiliogogogoch?" Jack repeated, without an instant's hesitation. "Why, that's where we have to deliver the eels or – "

"Or what?" said Alice, for he had come to an abrupt halt.

"Or else," he replied matter-of-factly (though he might also have been saying "or L's"). "It's a frightfully important dispatch for the Llanfairpwllgwyngyllgogery-chwyrndrobwllllantysiliogogogochians, you know," he added proudly.

"And what would happen if you failed to deliver them?" Alice ventured to ask.

"Oh, there's absolutely no chance of that!" Jack replied, with a carefree laugh. "Of course," he went on after a pause, "if anything *were* to happen to us – absolutely no chance of it, you understand – barely worth mentioning – but if it did – I say, *if* it did – why then, it'd be up to you to make the delivery."

Alice could not help thinking to herself how easily all the creatures she met assumed she would prove both willing and able to assist them, and she didn't know whether she ought to feel flattered or put upon. But they had reached the top of the hill by then, and once again Jack and Jill filled the pail up at the well.

The very moment they began their descent, however,

Jack tripped over his stick legs and proceeded to tumble, head over heels, with Jill naturally following after. Fortunately, Alice had been standing close by just in case such an accident occurred, and though she was unable to prevent the fall, at the very last moment she seized the pail from Jack, and so nimbly that no water spilled out of it. Though she was slightly anxious for his condition – had he really broken his crown this time, she wondered, and, if so, could it be mended? – she trusted that Jill would minister to him; and holding the pail carefully with both hands, she set off for – for the place named by Jack.

She did not have far to search. Almost immediately she spied a finger-post – to be exact, the beginning of the longest finger-post she had ever come across. Indeed, Alice could scarcely imagine how long it might be, for its other end seemed to be enshrouded in mist, so far off did it appear. The letters printed on it were *very* wide apart, as she began to read

CHAPTER VI

LOST-IN-A-MAZE-MENT

"L L A N F A I R P W L L G W Y N G Y L L G O -
GERYCHWYRNDROBWLLLLANTYSILIO-
GOGOGOCH – " Alice could only make out the other
end of the finger-post by cupping her hand over her
brow, half closing her eyes, and peering as hard as
possible into the distance, just like a sea-captain.
"Well!" she remarked in some amazement. "It must be
simply miles and miles long!" (By that, she meant
several hundred yards at least.) "And it's no wonder
that so many L's are used up here. Why, I count two –
four – six – ten – no, *eleven* for the place-name alone.
And I've got the strongest feeling that when I come to
the end of the post – if *ever* I do – I shall have arrived at
the place itself!"

For the moment, there was nothing to be done but continue in the direction which the letters indicated; and as the day was a very hot and sunny one, and the pailful of eels seemed to grow a little heavier with every step she took, Alice was soon so out of breath that she had to pause for a few moments each time she came to another L.

It was while resting at the ninth L that she was startled to hear a sharp bark just behind her: turning round, she saw a puppy, crouching in such a position as to be ready either to spring towards her or away from her at the slightest hint of danger. "Unless I'm very much mistaken," said Alice to herself, "this is the same little puppy the Italian Hairdresser used to brush the Grampus's gown." And since she had now become quite accustomed to speaking to all the creatures she met, she immediately said to the puppy in a friendly voice, exactly as if she were addressing another human being, "I beg your pardon, but would you please tell me whether I have much further to go before I am – " (pointing to the finger-post) " – here?"

Instead of answering her, however, the puppy merely cocked its head to one side, as if to express that it would understand her if it could, but since it couldn't, it didn't; then it barked again, though not too fiercely.

Thinking it mightn't have heard her clearly, Alice took a few steps forward and was about to repeat her question, when the puppy wagged its tail furiously and, barking, darted off a little way, turned round to face her again, and warily stared up at her. Its tongue was hanging out of its mouth, in which position it seemed so *very* long, that Alice wondered how such a small creature ever managed to pack it comfortably inside.

"I'm beginning to think," she said, looking at it in great perplexity, "you *are* a puppy, after all. I mean, you're *only* a puppy. You wo'n't speak, or answer back, or make rude personal remarks about all sorts of things, the way the other creatures do hereabouts!"

And the more Alice thought about it, the more curious it began to seem that she should actually encounter a *real* animal – "just as curious as having a moth or – or a mammoth – sitting beside me on the omnibus at home!" (Alice did not know exactly what a mammoth was, but she felt certain that it would not be allowed on to an omnibus.) Meanwhile, the puppy appeared to be waiting expectantly for Alice's next move; but though she looked here and there for a stick that it might fetch, there were none, "except for Jack and Jill, of course," she added with a mischievous smile, "and I'm not at all sure they would enjoy being fetched in a puppy's mouth."

Besides, her immediate concern was to reach her destination, and as she was already at the ninth L, with only two more left, she did not have much further to walk: so, lifting up the pail, she continued on her way. Not long afterwards, indeed, she arrived at the end of the finger-post. Just beyond it there was an immensely tall iron-grille gateway framed on each side by an equally tall hedge, and the top of the grille formed an arch, on which the word "LLABYRINTH" was marked in large letters.

"Now that's another word for a Maze," said Alice, "like the one we visited at Hampton Court – except that there's a letter too many. How fond they are of L's here!"

She peered through the iron grille, and what she saw on the other side was a narrow, shady path forking off to the left and an exactly similar one to the right: both of them were bordered by high, dark green hedges. "It certainly looks like a Maze," thought Alice; "and how cool and inviting it seems."

The iron gate stood ajar; there was nobody to tell her

that she was Trespassing on Private Property; so, after only a moment's hesitation, Alice stepped inside.

*   *   *   *   *

*   *   *   *

*   *   *   *   *

No sooner had she taken up a place in front of the two divergent paths, than she heard a mighty creak; and she was just in time to see the gate swing shut behind her. Alice immediately tried to open it again, but no matter how much she *argued* with the latch, taking it by the scruff of the neck, as she imagined, and giving it a good shake, it remained quite *firm*, just as firm as if it were a real person refusing to let her in. Whether she liked it or not, Alice was locked inside the Maze, and the thing to do now, clearly, was find its centre.

With her chin resting in the hollow between her thumb and her index finger, and her brow furrowed in a frown of concentration, she set her mind to the difficult question of which of the two paths she ought to take. "Let me see," she began, and she tried to recall everything she knew about Mazes. "If I keep turning to the left, I'll be all right – but if I keep turning to the right, I'll be left – left inside the Maze!" And though she was left wondering if indeed she was right (if you are able to follow *me*), she decided that she would adopt the first rule. "If I *should* lose my way," she added, as an afterthought, "why, I can always use my needle, for they do say a needle gives directions" (though she would have been quite at a loss to explain how).

Alice cautiously entered the Maze by the leftward path, and, keeping to the left, turned once, twice – only to find herself outside again at the third bend. "Hum," she murmured to herself, "it doesn't appear to be *that*, anyway. What if I were to take only right turns?" Which she did – alas! with exactly the same result. Alice was now very cross indeed. "At Hampton Court it wasn't at all like this – there the difficulty was to make your way *out*, not *in*! Well, you may do your worst," she cried, raising her fist at the tall hedges, "I mean to get in nevertheless!"

This time, when she re-entered the Maze by the left turning, Alice was surprised to see, at the place where the path divided in two, a large signpost which she was positive had not been there before, as it was surely the first thing she would have noticed. All it said, however, when she hurried over to read it, was "THIS WAY? OR THAT WAY?", and underneath were marked two arrows pointing in opposite directions. "Well, of all things!" she exclaimed, stamping her foot on the ground, so provoked did she feel. "That's not what I call a signpost! It ought to be answering the question, not asking it!"

Since it was of no help to her, Alice decided to take the path to the right: there again, she came upon a post at the fork. On this was marked the word "HITHER", its arrow pointing in one direction, and the word "THITHER", its arrow pointing in the other. "If all the signposts are going to be like these," she thought, "I shall just have to make my own mind up. But would I prefer to go Hither or Thither?" she wondered, though the question seemed so meaningless. "Now Hither does sound a little closer than Thither, and even if I don't know what it is, it might be an advantage to get there sooner, you know. On the other hand, Thither sounds more interesting, somehow, and perhaps no human being has ever set foot on it before. Then I'd become a sort of explorer, and I might even make it one of our colonies, except that I haven't got a flag with me, and explorers always plant the flag in new-discovered lands; and perhaps I'd crown myself Queen Alice the First – though being Governor-General would be *nearly* as nice – and rule over the Thitherians for thirty-three years, and of course declare war on the Hitherians unless they came bearing gifts and agreed to sign a treaty, and – oh, but all this nonsense I'm talking isn't going to get me anywhere at all!''

So Thither it was to be. Alice turned to the left (which was the direction it happened to be in), walked a little way, and found yet another signpost. On it was written, in very ornate lettering, ''YOU ARE HERE'' – ''I don't need a signpost to tell me that!'' thought Alice – and underneath, in brackets, ''(ELSEWHERE 500 YARDS)''.

''Come, this is more like it,'' she said aloud, and she was quite cheered by its second message. ''Since I don't know where I am, I *must* be better off elsewhere.'' And as she began to walk in the direction in which the post was pointing, gently swinging the pail back and forth to the rhythm of her step, Alice found herself repeating the word over and over in a dreamy sort of way, until it sounded as queer as though it belonged to some foreign language. ''Elsewhere – Elsewhere – Elsewhere – Elsewhere – that's where Hamlet had his castle in Denmark, I think. How does it go? – 'To be or not to be, that is the question!' '' (Which was, in truth, the only line Alice knew out of Shakespeare's play, but I doubt if there are many little girls who know so much.) And, still more encouragingly, she soon passed another signpost, which said "ELSEWHERE 300 YARDS", then another after that, "150 YARDS", and then she turned a bend in the path and found one which read simply "ELSEWHERE".

Alice came to a halt and looked at the post. "Why, how is this possible?" she said, in a tone of extreme puzzlement. "How can I be here and elsewhere at the same time? Yet it all started sensibly enough: for when I set out from – " (Alice hesitated, when she realised where she had actually set out from) " – from Here," she resolutely went on, "I had exactly five hundred yards to go, and I know I followed the directions correctly, and came closer and closer – and now that I've arrived, I'm not Elsewhere at all, I'm – well, I'm *here!*" Indeed, carefully taking in her surroundings, she began to suspect that she'd done nothing but return to her point of departure, for didn't the hedges rear up in the same fashion on both sides, and wasn't there that same funny little twist to the path, and only the signpost – but when she looked again at the signpost, she discovered to her astonishment that it now read "YOU ARE HERE". There could no longer be any doubt about it – she was back in the place where she had started out.

It was almost too much for poor Alice. With the tears welling up in her eyes, she sat cross-legged on the path and began to feel *very* sorry for herself. Gradually, however, she realised that she was not alone in the Maze. For from some way off, yet remarkably clearly, she heard a voice that she recognised, crying " 'Elp! 'Elp!"

"Why, that's the Country Mouse, surely it is!" exclaimed Alice, as delightedly as if she had come upon one of her oldest and dearest friends. "But where can it be exactly?" she wondered; and holding her two hands around her mouth, she shouted "Halloo! Halloo!", in the general direction from which the Mouse's cries had come. Sure enough, her call was returned with an " 'Alloo! 'Alloo!" ("just like an echo with a Cockney accent," thought Alice, "and what good acrostics this Maze must have!" – though I think she meant 'acoustics'). But when she called again a moment later, the Mouse's reply sounded fainter than before, so that Alice was forced to conclude that it too had taken a wrong turning.

"Oh, what *am* I to do?" she wailed. Then she added, not more than half seriously, "At least the Country

Mouse might leave behind it a trail of dropped H's, like Hop o' My Thumb!" And though she had only intended to make a little joke in order to cheer herself up, it did help to give her an idea. Alice looked down into the pail, where the eels were squirming about so strangely, and joining together into so many squares and rectangles, they reminded her of a book of Euclid's Geometry which she had once lazily dipped into when having nothing better to do. "Perhaps – " she said to herself, "if I were to toss an eel over the hedge, somebody would find it, and come looking to help me."

Alice carefully put her hand into the pail of water and drew out one of the eels. When she held it up in front of her, however, she almost burst out laughing. It looked so peculiar, bent double as it was, and though it felt alive and wriggly when she touched it, she couldn't manage to straighten out the right angle which it formed, no matter how hard she tried.

"I *am* sorry to do this to you, little friend," said Alice to the unfortunate creature, "but I'm *pretty* sure somebody will catch you first, so you wo'n't get hurt." And with these words, she cast it as high into the air as she could and watched it disappear over the hedge.

"There it goes!" Alice cried out in a hopeful tone,

waiting expectantly for somebody to catch it. Before very long, however, the eel made a dramatic reappearance above the hedge and circled there several times as if uncertain which direction to take; then, after another moment or two, when it seemed to hover in mid-air, it suddenly began to return towards her at an alarming speed. If Alice had not quickly raised her arm to reach up and grab it, it would probably have sailed right past her and landed with a thump in the hedge opposite.

"Why, it's behaved just like a boomerang," she said in dismay: "which isn't surprising, the shape it is!" And since it would have been pointless to make another attempt, as they were all the same shape, Alice gently put the eel back into the pail and sat down again. There was only one thing left to try. But her needle, when she took it out of her pocket, did not know how to give directions at all, making Alice wonder how needles had ever acquired such a reputation; as for using it to return to her own room at home ("though that'd mean an end to all my adventures!" she thought sadly), why, however closely she brought its eye up to her face, she couldn't even get the tip of her nose through. So you see, she really didn't know what to do, and she just sat there, feeling very unhappy indeed.

Poor Alice! For if she'd only had a bird's-eye-view of the Maze,

she would have realised that by turning right and right again and yet again, three times in all, then turning left four times in a row, she would find herself at the centre.

"Well, I'm lost," said Alice simply: "there's no getting away from *that* – or from here!" she added in a melancholy voice. "I wonder if there's a word – what they call an abstract noun – for such a state of affairs: something like 'lost-in-a-maze-ment', I should think."

And, as she sat there, she began to grow so weary that her head nearly dropped on to her lap and, almost without realising it, she allowed her eyelids to close.

*   *   *   *   *
    *   *   *   *
*   *   *   *   *

A moment later, Alice was roused by the feeling that somebody or something had brushed close by her. She opened her eyes again, just in time to catch sight of a leg – or rather, a hairy white paw in a snugly fitting spat – disappearing round the next bend in the path.

Extremely annoyed at herself for having let pass the chance of joining forces with some other creature in the Maze, Alice got to her feet and hurried off in pursuit, quite forgetting the pail of eels which she had carried such a distance. When she turned the corner herself, however, all she could see was the bespatted paw about to disappear beyond the next one. And, the further she went on, soon losing count of the many twists and turns in the path, she never did see any more than that one part of the creature's body. At the same time, she became aware of a curious murmur, as of a distant waterfall. At least, it started as a murmur, then it gradually grew into a rumble, then into a roar – until Alice, who by now was running so fast that she wouldn't have been able to stop even if she had wished to, turned a final corner into the very centre of the Maze, which was, to her astonishment, filled up to bursting point with animals and birds of every description (and a number of quite indescribable ones as well).

CHAPTER VII

ALICE VOLUNTEERS

What a commotion there was! What dreadfully low spirits everybody seemed to be in! Alice had never in her life heard such groaning – and what distressed her most of all were the squeals of hunger from the littlest ones. "How long can they have been in here?" she wondered. "The poor things must be half starved!" But while she was squeezing through in order to make a comfortable place for herself (and it was not made easier for her, that there was an otter just beside her, which *would* choose now of all times to clean out its fur), a call for silence was heard; and Alice looked up to see a Welsh Rabbit, apparently a person of some prominence among them. She knew it was a Welsh Rabbit because it was holding a piece of toasted cheese in one paw and a bottle of Worcestershire Sauce in the other. Moreover, when she stood up on tiptoe, she noticed that, on its hind paws, it wore an elegant pair of spats, "and so that was the creature I followed in the Maze," she said to herself with satisfaction.

The groans having died down at last, the Rabbit began to speak, in a strong Welsh accent. "Listen, all of

you! I tell you straight – lost it is we are – and tired we
are – and hungry, too, and no mistake. So until as how
we decide upon a plan to save us, it's a race that I
propose!"

The response was immediate. Shouts of "No, no!",
"Never!", and "Nohow!" rose up from everywhere at
once.

"Carried unanimously, I see," the Welsh Rabbit
replied, with a complacent expression. (And nobody
could deny that it had been unanimous.) "But as we
ca'n't have a race without a Grand Prize," it went on,
"whoever wins it will receive a bite out of my toasted
cheese washed down by a refreshing draught of
Worcestershire Sauce."

On hearing this announcement, all the animals
eagerly crowded round the Rabbit wanting to be told
the rules.

"There will be three principal events," it said
pompously: "Running a Temperature, Jumping to
Conclusions, and Skipping the Difficult Passages. Are
you all ready?"

Shouts went up of "No!" and "Not yet!"

"Off you go, then!" cried the Welsh Rabbit.

Alice screamed with laughter to see the contestants at

their various races, so painfully intense did the expressions on their faces become: though she grew rather concerned about those who were competing in the Running a Temperature event, for their eyes were starting to bulge out of their heads, and some of them were starting to turn an unhealthy shade of crimson. Then she fancied (or fancied she fancied) that a Kangaroo nearby was leaping over this Difficult Passage:

> Knowledge is a coincidence between the association of ideas, and the order or succession of events or phenomena, according to the relation of cause and effect, and in whatever is subsidiary, or necessary to realise, approximate and extend such coincidence; understanding, by the relation of cause and effect, that order or succession, the development of which empowers an intelligent being, by means of one event or phenomenon, or by a series of given events or phenomena, to anticipate the recurrence of another related or unrelated series of events or phenomena.

"Come, take my hand," said the Kangaroo to Alice in a kindly voice, after alighting safely on the other side. "Because I see that we're about to turn a page, and that can be quite a frightening experience for one so young. Are you holding on tightly, child? Here we go —

– and upsadaisy!" the Kangaroo concluded, a little out
of breath. As to Alice, she could not be exactly sure for a
few moments what had happened to her. She had a
vague impression of a large white rectangle rearing up
before her, and, as she would tell her sister in wonder-
ment, "It felt like scaling the White Cliffs of Dover, you
know, or like a salmon leaping up a waterfall, and it was
really quite exhilarating, only it *was* a relief to have
arrived safely at the top of the following page!"

"Well now, my dear," said the Kangaroo, when it
had fully recovered its breath, "I *have* enjoyed making
your acquaintance, but it's high time I got back into the
race. Aren't you taking part in it at all?"

"Why," said Alice, very decidedly, "it's the silliest
race I ever saw!"

"Ah, Jumping to Conclusions, I see," said the
Kangaroo with a nod of approval. "Then let me wish
you the best of luck, child, in your chosen category. Oh,
do stop fidgeting, I say!" it added crossly.

"I beg your pardon?" said Alice, for the Kangaroo's
sudden change of tone had caught her by surprise, the
more so because she certainly hadn't been fidgeting.

"Oh, it wasn't to you I was speaking, my dear," the
Kangaroo hastily assured her, with a friendly little pat

on the head. "It was my babies, you understand." And it held open a wide, roomy pocket in its front, in which Alice could see two very young kangaroos, peering up at her with large round eyes. "The little darlings get so restless when they're obliged to stay indoors. It quite wears me out!"

"Here, Ma, when are we going to eat?" cried one of them in an impatient voice.

"Hush, Montmorency!" said the Kangaroo. "Mother is trying to win us all some nice toasted cheese."

"Don't like toasted cheese!" said the other baby, rather ungratefully, thought Alice.

"Just you think about all the hungry little kangaroos in Australia – and I promise you you'll like it!" was its mother's sensible reply. Then, waving goodbye to Alice, it hopped away in search of Difficult Passages.

The race had gone on for about a quarter of an hour, when the Welsh Rabbit suddenly called a halt by shouting "Stop!" at the top of its voice. Whereupon everybody collapsed together in a heap, their little chests heaving with exhaustion.

It was no easy matter deciding which was the winner, as there had been three separate types of events, and the ground had been so packed with competitors, it was nearly impossible to see straight; but, in the end, the Rabbit chose a tall and extremely thin Loon, which had managed to run its temperature up to 162°. To cheers from the others the Loon stepped forward to receive its Prize: it took a great bite out of the toasted cheese, which it greedily devoured; then it swallowed a mouthful from the bottle of Worcestershire Sauce, which caused it to turn a colour no loon has *ever* been seen outside of a painting-book, "and it must have made its temperature rise even higher!" thought Alice.

"Well now, brothers," said the Welsh Rabbit: "after such an exciting race, what would be better than a riddle – a riddle, look you, so hard, so devilishly complicated, none of you will ever be able to solve it!"

Though Alice preferred her riddles just a little easier than that, she was greatly fond of them in general, and paid close attention to the Welsh Rabbit. And when all the creatures had settled down at last, it began (telling the riddle as a poem whose form Alice could not help feeling she had heard somewhere before):

ALICE VOLUNTEERS

"I knew an ancient sea-dog
   Whose name was Peg-Leg Ned:
He steered his ship around the world
   While standing on his head:
'I use my toes for signalling
   In semaphore,' he said.

When Ned sat down to take a meal,
   The fare was of the best:
A dozen oysters on a dish,
   A crab he nicely dressed,
And as a special birthday treat,
   Crow's eggs from the crow's nest.

'Such mounds of food,' thought Peg-Leg Ned,
  'Are far too much for me:
With crab, and eggs, and oysters, too,
  There's quite enough for three.
I shall invite my dearest friends
  To come and share my tea.'

'Then row ashore and fetch before
  The turning of the tide
The Grampus and the Hairdresser!'
  Ned to his boatswain cried.
'How shall I recognise them, sir?'
  Was all the youth replied.

'The Grampus, first,' his Captain said,
  'Is very like a whale.
It wears a long professor's gown
  Hooped with a farthingale,
A mortar-board upon its head,
  Two flappers and a tail.

'As to its friend, the Hairdresser,
  He stands at four foot three;
His hair is black and curly, for
  He comes from Italy;
A waxed moustache adorns his face –
  A gentleman is he.'

ALICE VOLUNTEERS

So off to town the boatswain went,
  And scanned the busy scene;
But though he searched both high and low,
  And also in between,
The Grampus and the Hairdresser
  Were nowhere to be seen.

When suddenly, along the street,
  He spied two creatures walking –
Of ale – and ants – and ambergris
  Animatedly talking –
And which they would prefer to find
  Inside their Christmas stocking.

'It must be they!' the youth exclaimed;
  'It must – or I'm undone!
For Peg-Leg Ned will have my head
  If I return alone!'
And peering close from left to right,
  He scrutinised each one.

The first, alas, in shape and size
  Was nohow like a whale.
He wore no long professor's gown
  Hooped with a farthingale,
No mortar-board upon his head,
  Nor any such detail.

The second, his companion, stood
  At near twice *four foot three;*
His hair could not be black, because
  He had no hair, you see;
No waxed moustache adorned his face –
  No gentleman was he.

And this is how my riddle ends,
  Its hero in despair:
Yet he might well have spotted them,
  If he had shown more care.
The Grampus and the Hairdresser
  Were both in town – but where?"

The Welsh Rabbit looked at them all with a gleeful expression on its face. "*There*'s a riddle for you, now," it said: "one to while away the hours and hours and hours!" And it asked "Any ideas?", in a voice that was confident nobody would be able to answer it. The creatures, indeed, appeared for the moment to have forgotten the predicament they were in, as they concentrated on finding the solution.

However, it was Alice who raised a hand first, after a pause of only a minute or so.

"Yes, dear?" said the Welsh Rabbit with an

indulgent smile, as though to say, "It is, of course, but a child – but let us humour her."

"Well," said Alice carefully, "it seems obvious to me – " (a beginning which this time caused not only the Rabbit but all the other animals to smile: one or two of the younger ones tittered audibly) " – that the two creatures that the boatswain met in the street were *really* the Grampus and the Hairdresser, only he looked at the second one first, you know, and the first one second."

The Welsh Rabbit's indulgent smile faded from its face in double quick time, and there was a long silence. Then, when even the very dullest among those present had tested Alice's solution and discovered it to be the correct one, everybody turned to glare at her, so that she began to wish she had not spoken at all.

"Why, that riddle ought to have been good for three hours at least," remarked an old Owl with disgust, "and there she's gone and gobbled it up at once, the greedy thing!"

"Some people just ca'n't help being spoil-sports!" snapped an Ostrich, pulling its head out of the earth.

"But – how can a riddle be spoilt by somebody answering it?" asked a bewildered Alice. "For surely, that's what riddles are for?"

"Oh, you haven't understood anything!" the Owl replied. "Now we've nothing to think about again except how hungry we all are!", and it rudely hooted at Alice.

"Be quiet!" the Welsh Rabbit suddenly called out. "I know of something that'll soon put you off thinking about food. I have volunteered the Otter to sing us a song. And if any of you have ever heard the Otter's singing voice, you'll know that not even Miss Know-All here – " (a remark which caused Alice to turn a deep red) " – will be able to spoil *that*!"

"My song," said the Otter, after it had stepped forward and faced the assembly, "tells of an Otter – but you mustn't make the mistake of thinking that that

Otter is myself. It is, as you might say, a composite Otter, the Platonic ideal of Otters, the very essence of Otterdom. Oh, and there's a Hamster also," it added, in a far less enthusiastic tone. Then it began:

"*An Otter and a Hamster*
Agreed to build a dam
Of weeds, and beads, and caraway seeds,
And pots of damson jam.

'Let's call it Otterdam, sir,'
Said the Otter with a wink.
'Otterdam, sir?' said the Hamster:
'No – Hamsterdam, I think.'

The argument grew hotter
On how to name the dam.
'For an Otter you're a rotter!'
Was the Hamster's epigram.

'To call it Hamsterdam, sir,
Would clearly be absurd –
It sounds too much like double Dutch!'
Was the Otter's final word.

Said the Hamster, 'Why, I oughter – ',
And it took the damson jam,
Poured a pot o'er the poor Otter,
Who loudly cried out, 'Dam – ' "

"*Thank* you," the Welsh Rabbit interrupted it, "but that'll be enough of that! Not at all suitable!"

The Otter crept back to its place where it could be heard mumbling, "Oh dear! They never understand – what the Otter in my song meant to say was 'Dam the river by yourself, if you must, but don't look to me to assist you.'" It was so disappointed, that Alice took pity on it, saying, "Well, I thought it a very charming song – and *beautifully* sung."

"How kind of you to say so," the Otter thanked her. "Perhaps you'd like to have my Ottergraph?"

"Why, yes," said Alice (who wondered how it spelt the word), "I'd like that very much. I'm afraid, though, I haven't got a pen and album with me."

"It's of little consequence," the Otter replied. "I ca'n't write, anyway."

Thinking it might be wiser to change the subject, Alice said, "Instead of running silly races and asking riddles, you know, we should all be trying harder to find a way out of the Maze.'

"We-ll," said the Otter, "there *is* a way, though it may be dreadfully dangerous."

"I *knew* there must be one!" cried Alice. "Do tell me what it is!"

"If you turn your head, you'll notice just behind you a large hole in the ground." (Alice drew back in some alarm, as she had been standing on its very rim.) "Now – there are two Schools of Thought about that hole," the Otter went on, adopting a learned manner. "One School claims that it'll eventually lead out of the Maze, if you crawl far enough along it. The other that it doesn't lead anywhere at all, and simply goes on and on, to Infinity. But, you see, since no one has ever returned to tell the tale, no one knows which is right."

"What is needed is a volunteer," remarked Alice, looking down into the depths of the hole, which was so dark she made nothing out at all.

"Did you say 'I should like to be a volunteer'?" the Otter anxiously asked.

"No, I didn't," replied Alice. "What I said was – " She did not have the opportunity to complete her sentence, however, as they had been overheard, and there suddenly arose shrill cries of "A volunteer! A volunteer! The child wishes to volunteer!"

"Why no, I – " Alice attempted to explain, " – I only said that *somebody* ought – " But it was all in vain, so loud did the clamour grow around them (for word of the volunteer was now beginning to spread through the crowd); and as the creatures bore down upon her, so that they quite blotted out the sky, she found herself backing closer and closer to the large, gaping hole – until she was shoved once too often and tumbled in with a scream. Alice had been *volunteered*.

She had one last glimpse of the Otter peering over the edge, before she plunged deep into the hole, which was, she discovered, a long tunnel running horizontally. But though its walls were very close together (which was something she *felt* only, as she could not see them), she advanced so gracefully – almost as if she were falling sideways – that she never bruised herself against them. Once, when her body made an awkward wriggle, and she seemed about to hit the wall, she had the distinct impression that it drew back hastily to make room for her, "just like a living thing!"

Alice continued in this way for several minutes, and she soon became convinced that the School of Thought, which believed the tunnel led on to Infinity, was right.

"Infinity, now," she said to herself in a thoughtful voice: "all I know about it is that it looks like an 8 that was so tired, it simply *had* to lie down and take a nap. And it's where parallel lines meet, isn't it, and what a queer sight that must be! I wonder how they greet one

another after such a long separation. Most people say 'Isn't it a small world!' but that wouldn't do at all. They'd say 'Isn't it a *large* world', rather." And Alice (for she had nothing better to occupy herself with) began to imagine the First Parallel Line greeting the Second Parallel Line with "Bless my soul, fancy meeting you here!" To which the Second would say "Why, I haven't seen you since I ran alongside you in that dog-eared old Parallelogram on Page 138 of *Todhunter*!" Then the First Parallel Line would come back with "Remember how we used to wave across at each other? I never thought the day would come when I'd actually get to meet you!"

"It *is* true," thought Alice, turning the matter over in her mind, "that if I really do reach Infinity, all the numbers will be abolished, so there'll be no Multiplication-Tables, which I ca'n't say I'll mind too much, and no Addition, Subtraction, and Division, either – but then, it must mean that Time will be abolished as well, and there'll be no breakfasts, dinners, or teas, and no seasons, and nobody'll grow any the older but stay the same age for, oh, ages and ages, which might be nice, except that I'd prefer to be *just* a little more grown-up than I am now, and there'll be no – " and here, whistling through the tunnel, the word 'no' echoed back at her, only longer and more drawn-out as if all the little 'o's that were in it had been laid end to end to form a tunnel of their own: 'Noooooooooo!' – "it's a bit like multiplying 'no' by ten, and then multiplying the result by ten, and then multiplying *that*, and so forth," said Alice to herself, and, inside her head, she saw it written down clearly as 'No,ooo,ooo,ooo' – "and it's the answer I shall give, next time they tell me to go to bed before I've quite finished playing, and they wo'n't know what to say to *that*, I'm sure, and – "

But, before Alice could utter another word, she spied a light at the end of the tunnel, a light which grew larger and larger until it seemed to be rushing towards her, and all of a sudden there she was – out in the open air.

CHAPTER VIII

QUEUEING

Alice sprang out of the tunnel like a rocket, and so fast that she actually hovered in the air for a second or two before falling to earth – quite painlessly. While she was getting her breath back, however, and dusting off her clothes, she heard a voice that she recognised cry out, "Oh *no*, you don't, young lady! You aren't going to steal a place in *this* queue as easily as that!" And a second voice, which also struck her as familiar, remarked, in a tone that sounded very ill-tempered, "Just because she falls out of the sky on top of us, she seems to think she's entitled to special treatment! That would be *too* easy!" And the first voice concluded, "Why, if we allowed her to have her way this once, the next thing you know, everybody would go about doing the same!"

When Alice jumped up on to her feet at last, she discovered that she had landed in the middle of a little queue of people; and what surprised her most of all was that she was squeezed in between none other than the Red Queen and the White Queen, whom she had last known in Looking-Glass Land, "and I'm certain I only dreamt them *then*," she wondered, "so how is it possible that they're here *now*?"

So astonished was she at finding them, she forgot at first that there exists a whole set of rules for speaking to Queens. "What are you two doing here?" she bluntly asked them; hastily adding, " – your Majesties", for fear that they might have been offended. And, indeed, the two Queens only stared haughtily at her, as if to say that if nobody had any objection, they would as soon be offended as anything else.

"Come now, surely you remember," said Alice, smiling encouragingly at each of them in turn: "my name is Alice. We all met together on the Eighth Square of Looking-Glass Land, for I had become a Queen myself by then, and I invited you to come to my dinner-party – that's to say," she corrected herself, "you both invited each other – and such a grand time of it we had."

Though neither of them made any reply, the Red Queen nodded her head in assent, while the White Queen smiled warmly at Alice.

"Oh, I'm glad, you *do* remember!" said Alice (who had often wondered whether the creatures in her dreams remembered being in them as well as she remembered dreaming them).

"Nothing of the kind!" replied the Red Queen.

"But you nodded, just as if – " Alice began to say.

"Not I!" said the Red Queen. "I may have rocked my head back and forth in a vertical direction, but that's not at all what I call nodding."

"I suppose you think *I* smiled!" the White Queen screamed at Alice. "It's a fine thing when a person ca'n't even let her mouth widen across her face in the shape of a crescent, thereby causing her teeth to be bared, without all and sundry – " ("Especially sundry!" the Red Queen interjected) " – accusing her of having smiled!"

"The impudence of the creature!" said the Red Queen again. "Why, in all the time I've known you, you've only smiled once – and I must say, you couldn't have been more apologetic about it."

Alice decided that none of this was leading anywhere,

and she took advantage of the lull in their conversation to try and find out what they were queueing for. As far as she could make out, the queue was stretched tight between two little wooden buildings, one at either end: they were identical, each with its slanting roof and its single window formed like an upturned U, making it resemble an oversized dog kennel. Alice and the two Queens were standing just at the half-way position.

Hoping the Red Queen was now feeling a little calmer, Alice politely asked her, "Have you been queueing here long?"

"That's a stupid question!" was all the answer she received.

"Well, *I* ca'n't see what's stupid about it," said Alice, with more spirit.

"I thought everybody knew the answer to that one," said the Red Queen, shaking her head at Alice's ignorance.

"Consider, my dear," said the White Queen, and she looked inconsolably sad: "she's still very young."

"As a matter of fact, child," said the Red Queen, turning to Alice, "a minute ago her White Majesty and I were in the middle of doing handstands while balancing flag-poles on the ends of our noses, but of course the

moment we saw you come, we cried to each other 'Act normally!' and simply made up this quiet little queue. That's what always happens when you go somewhere different, you know: whatever the inhabitants are about just before you arrive, they immediately stop it and start doing something quite ordinary, so as not to alarm a complete stranger. And the moment you leave, naturally, they start up again. Surely you knew that?"

"No-o," said Alice thoughtfully: "though I *have* sometimes fancied it was so – for instance, when I pass through a town or village I haven't been to before."

"Well, now you've been told, commit it to memory," said the White Queen; and the two Queens began to whisper together with sarcastic little smiles in Alice's direction.

As you can imagine, Alice did not care for that one bit, and said so sharply. "It's generally considered *very* rude to whisper in company, you know!"

"And who was whispering, may I ask?" said the White Queen, all innocence.

"*You* were, of course."

"*I*? *Whispering*? Just because I lowered my voice to a barely audible hiss!" said the White Queen in an indignant tone. "Why, I've never been so insulted in all my life!"

"Oh, please, please, your Majesty," pleaded Alice, for the White Queen in her fury had gone so red-faced, she could hardly be told apart from the Red Queen, "you mustn't lose your temper with me. I only thought – "

The White Queen interrupted her. "I *never* lose my temper – not since I had it attached to my skirt on a nice little chain. I used to, though, all the time," she added wistfully.

"Oh, she used to!" the Red Queen repeated with emphasis. "Her temper or her gloves! It was either one or the other thing – and often both at once! If she lost her temper, you see, she'd lose her gloves; and when she lost her gloves, *how* she'd lose her temper! It was at my suggestion, you know, that she got the chain."

"Oh, was it?" said Alice, who would very much have liked to peek at the White Queen's temper, except that she feared it would not be civil of her. Instead, as the queue had been gradually moving forward, and they had almost reached the little window, she said, "I nearly forgot to ask: what is it you're queueing for?"

"I don't know, I'm sure," the White Queen airily replied. "I've never come close enough to see what there is for sale."

"Well, we're about to find out, I think," said Alice to herself, "for there's only one customer ahead of us now."

Just as it came their turn, however, the window was slammed shut, and a cardboard sign inserted in it, which read "CLOSED – APPLY AT WINDOW OPPOSITE". Whereupon everybody briskly turned in the other direction, which meant that Alice and the two Queens found themselves at the very end of the queue.

"But that's unjust!" said Alice crossly. "Now we'll have longer than ever to wait!"

To her surprise, the two Queens, usually such irritable creatures, accepted this change as though nothing could be more natural. "I daresay you've not had much experience of queues yet," was all the Red Queen would reply.

"Where I come from," Alice ventured to say, "they only move in one direction."

"What a waste of a good queue!" said the Red Queen. "That'd be like a stairway that only went up, not down."

"It'd be like a book that could only be read from left to right, not right to left." the White Queen added.

Alice was on the point of replying that that was the only sort of book *she* knew, but she thought better of it, and they all fell silent for a minute or two. Then, feeling that there could be no safer subject for a conversation than the weather, she broke the silence by remarking,

"It's a very pleasant day, don't you agree?"

"For December – yes," said the Red Queen.

"So it *is* December here, too!" said Alice excitedly. "I was wondering, you see."

"I don't know what you mean by 'too'," the Red Queen replied, "but of course it isn't December! Who ever saw such a sky and such a sun in December?"

"But you just said it *was* a pleasant day for December," Alice replied in a puzzled voice.

"Well, wouldn't it be?" said the Red Queen. "But this month is August – and it's a perfectly commonplace day for August."

Though Alice found talking to the Queens an exhausting business, she had at least learned the month of the year, which she believed was always a useful piece of information to have at one's fingertips. And, as she was determined not to make the mistake again of starting the conversation, she merely stood by, looking at them both with a half smile on her face, one that could have meant almost anything at all.

Soon afterwards, they reached the little window on the far side; and yet, here too, just as they were preparing to inspect whatever goods might be on display, it closed in their faces with a slam, and the same cardboard sign re-appeared: "CLOSED – APPLY AT WINDOW OPPOSITE". Of course everybody changed direction as before.

"Oh, this is too much!" cried Alice, who, though a very well-mannered little girl, was becoming more and more impatient. "Here I am – at the end of the queue all over again!"

The Red Queen remained as serene about the matter as she had been the first time round. "Are you good at spelling, child?" she asked, with an irritating smirk.

"I think I am," Alice said cautiously.

"Then you ought to know that a *queue* is always followed by *you!*" At this remark the two Queens screamed with laughter, and fell into such fits, they had to hug each other to keep upright.

"That's a very poor joke, I'm afraid," said an unsmiling Alice.

The Red Queen spluttered, that was how angry she was. "Why, if I thought for a moment I had made a – a – " (she could scarcely bring herself to pronounce the word) " – a *joke*, I'd have to wash my mouth out with soap and water!"

"She would, too," the White Queen added, " – and only the best imported soap."

"I'm sorry," said Alice defiantly, "but it still sounded like a joke to me."

The two Queens looked at each other: the White Queen let out a little gasp, and the Red Queen remarked with a grim expression, "The brazen creature has *ever* so much to learn about speaking to her elders and betters! It reminds me of the old nursery rhyme – you remember, my dear:

> *"Alice, Alice, full of malice,*
> *How she loves to smash the palace!*
> *Silver on the table, gold upon the chair,*
> *Alice in the kitchens pulling Tweeny's hair!"*

"Oh my, yes," said the White Queen, wringing her hands, "it's her to the life!"

"Why, I never heard of such a nursery rhyme," said Alice.

"Ah, that's because yours wasn't a *royal* nursery, you see," explained the Red Queen. "This rhyme is By Appointment To Their Majesties."

"Poor, poor infant!" sighed the White Queen. "With her upbringing, is it any wonder she's so rude and ignorant? Ah well, it was ever thus!"

"Now, if you'll excuse us," the Red Queen said to

Alice; "life ca'n't be all fun, you know."

They had been so busy criticising her, that it was only now Alice noticed that the queue of customers (if indeed that is what they were) had become shorter and shorter, so that the only ones left were the two Queens and herself. Even more surprising, the little window did not close this time, and the Red Queen set to bargaining furiously with somebody on the other side of it. Alas! though she was curious to find out what was happening, and would stand on tiptoe and peer over the Queens' shoulders, Alice could hardly make anything out at all – the more so, as the counter was gradually becoming encumbered with parcels of every kind: large square ones, small oblong ones, and medium-sized ones which bulged out of every corner.

At last the two Queens came away, so laden down that Alice could just about see the tops of their crowns. As they happily trotted off, the Red Queen turned to her, saying, "Always remember, child. Dot your i's and cross your t's, mind your p's and q's, and the other letters'll take care of themselves!" – and they were gone.

$$* \qquad * \qquad * \qquad * \qquad *$$
$$* \qquad * \qquad * \qquad *$$
$$* \qquad * \qquad * \qquad * \qquad *$$

But when it was Alice's own turn at the little window, she discovered that it had closed again, and the sign had gone up. "Bother!" she could not help saying aloud. "What sort of shop is it that wo'n't stay open for more than a minute at a time!" Nevertheless, she dutifully applied at the window opposite, only to find that there too, just as she stepped up to it, it decided to close down. ("And I'm positive they do it on purpose!" thought Alice.) So then she hurried back to the first, which also closed an instant before she had time to make any inquiry – then to the second – then back to the first again – and now faster and faster, so that the windows slamming each in their turn began to sound like photographic plates being shut into a camera.

"Well, if they don't wish to sell me anything," said poor Alice, who was quite out of breath from running back and forth, "I'm sure I don't care to buy anything!"

" 'Afternoon, m'dear, and what can I do for you?" a soft voice was heard nearby, and though it was dreadfully faint and far-off sounding, it startled Alice quite as much as if somebody had just screamed in her ear. Looking up, she realised to her great astonishment that one of the little shop windows was now actually open; but even when she strained to peer over the top, she could not make out anybody serving behind it, and the voice, when it spoke again, seemed to come from somewhere very low and deep within.

When she had got over her first surprise, Alice reflected a moment. "Let me see – " she started to say.

"Sorry," said the voice again, "we don't stock spectacles!"

"No, I meant – "

"No dictionaries, either!"

"Perhaps," said Alice politely, "it would be better if you told me what you *do* sell."

"Anything your heart desires," the voice dreamily replied.

"In that case," ventured Alice, "I'll take just what the Red Queen bought."

"Heavens, we're all out of *those*!" said the voice. "Such a run on 'em to-day, there was."

"Then I'd like – "

"Wo'n't have any in till the week after next. *And* they're already very heavily subscribed."

"Well then, have you any – "

" 'Fraid not. No call for 'em these days, y'see. You *are* the unlucky one, aren't you?"

Alice hesitated. "What about – " she began to ask.

"No indeed!" said the voice in indignation. "I haven't stocked those since a customer choked on one. Went quite puce, as I recall."

Alice had never in her life felt such frustration. But the further she went on, the greater became her determination to buy something – anything at all – just so she could take it back with her. And it suddenly occurred to her that most such little shops do duty as post offices: so, taking a deep breath, and speaking so quickly that the words all rushed out together, she said, "Idverymuchliketobuyapostagestampplease!"

"Why, of course, m'dear," came the voice in a soothing tone. "It's natural you'd want to send a letter home from hereabouts – a nice manly M, perhaps, or one of those curly S's. Very popular, S's are. Would you like me to wrap the stamp for you? I ought to warn you, though – if it's to be a present, it'll be rather awkward removing the price."

"No thank you," said Alice, though she *was* tempted to see what it would look like in wrapping-paper, "it wo'n't be necessary."

"Just as you like," said the voice. "But perhaps you'd prefer to have it delivered?"

"No again," Alice replied, trying hard not to laugh, "I'll just carry it with me."

"Oh, what it is to be young and spry!" it sighed. "Ah me, my time'll come."

"I'm afraid I don't quite understand you," said Alice.

"Well, m'dear, if you'd just like to take a look through the window," said the voice, "you will observe that I am – I mean that I *was* – a caterpillar."

Alice wasted no time in peering down into the gloom, but all she could see inside the shop was one little wooden chair on which sat a waxy black ball, and what it meant she did not understand at first. Then suddenly it came to her, and she exclaimed, "Why, of course, you've turned into a chrysalis, haven't you!" ("And no wonder its voice seemed to come from so far away," she thought to herself.)

"We caterpillars, y'see," it went on, as painfully as if it were struggling to get the words out, "enjoy a privilege unique in nature: To be given our old age first, so that, enriched by the wisdom of experience, we may then live our youth to the full. And I have the feeling – " (here the Caterpillar's voice became *very* strained) " – I most distinctly have the feeling – that my own youth is nearly upon me!"

No sooner had it spoken these words, than the chrysalis began to crack open, "just as though one were unwrapping a rainbow for Christmas," thought Alice: and from within it there emerged the most exquisitely graceful butterfly she had ever seen. A trifle unsteadily, it fluttered out through the window; then, as it flew off, plying its little wings upwards with ever more ease, Alice heard it call out to her in a high, silvery, child-like voice, "Don't forget your postage-stamp!"

CHAPTER IX

SWAN PIE AND GREENS

Alice picked up the postage-stamp from off the counter and peered at it with great interest. Though it depicted a King's head ("I know they mean to pay tribute to monarchs by displaying their heads so," she would think when looking at any postage-stamp, "yet it always makes them seem as if they've just been beheaded!"), it was so tiny, she could not make out which King it belonged to. So she held it up for a closer look; but even though she expected it now to appear larger in her eyes, for that is what perspective does to objects, she could not help thinking it was growing out of *all* proportion. Indeed, before she had had the time to realise what was happening, it had shot up to such a height that she could scarcely see over the top, "and surely that *is* contrary to the Laws of Perspective!" she said to herself.

So startled was Alice by the turn of events, she was tempted to let the stamp go at once: only she discovered that she was no longer standing in front of the counter as before but sitting at a neatly laid-out table in a little garden. When she looked one way, she saw what seemed to be an inn, with a thatched roof and honeysuckle-covered walls; in the other direction, flowed a little brook; and standing over her was an aged Frog dressed as a waiter, and with a waiter's pencil and pad at the ready. There was another seat opposite hers, but it was unoccupied: so that when the Frog, with a supercilious expression on its face, suddenly croaked, "I suppose you *are* ready to order at last," Alice knew it must be speaking to her.

She looked again at the thing she was still holding in her hand. Naturally, the size it had become, it wasn't now to be thought of as a postage-stamp. Even so, Alice was a little surprised to find that it had meanwhile turned into a menu card, at the top of which was inscribed the name of the establishment: THE KING'S HEAD. Alice had lots of questions which she wanted to ask, but after all her adventures she was becoming *very* tired and hungry, and she simply couldn't remember when last she had eaten anything. But though her first thought was "I haven't any idea of the time of day, or whether it ought to be breakfast, lunch, or dinner, so how shall I know what I feel like ordering?", this hardly mattered in the end, as the menu turned out to be written all in French.

Alice looked up apologetically at the Frog-Waiter. "I don't know French well enough to read your menu, I'm afraid."

Without a word, the Frog took the menu card, turned it the other way up, and handed it back to her. Read that way, it was clearly written out in English. "*Well!* I never realised before that French was only English upside-down," thought Alice to herself. "What a difference that's going to make to lessons from now on! Mademoiselle will be quite amazed at my progress!" Unfortunately, though, it was covered over with so many stains, she still could not read it properly. So instead she decided to seek the Frog-Waiter's advice.

"What is your local speciality, if you please?" she asked, as she had once heard grown-ups do.

"Bad table-manners," said the Frog, carelessly flicking a spelling bee away from the table with its napkin.

"So I observe," Alice murmured under her breath; for, looking hard at the table-cloth, she found there were just as many stains there. "I mean," she added: "is there a dish you think I would like?"

"We-ll," replied the Frog in a slow drawl, "what I *ca'n't* recommend is the Frog's Legs, you know. Order those – and you'll see as how the service slows down something dreadful."

"Thank you for telling me so," said Alice, "but I really hadn't thought of ordering such a – " Just then she noticed that the Frog had started to pay particular attention to what she was saying: so she went on " – such a rich delicacy as Frog's Legs."

The Frog smiled. Then, in a more friendly way, it said, "Can I tempt you with a slice of Humble Pie?"

"What exactly is in Humble Pie?" asked Alice.

"Oh, quite a few things!" came the answer. "There's treacle, French mustard, half a bottle of cod-liver oil, a tuppenny box of tin-tacks, and a pound of sultanas."

"That doesn't sound very nice," said Alice doubtfully.

"No – " the Frog agreed with some reluctance, "to be sure, it doesn't *sound* nice. But where food is concerned, you know, it's the taste that matters, not the sound."

"Perhaps so," Alice replied tactfully, "but it's not really what I feel like having to-day. And I ca'n't seem to make up my mind at all."

"Then I'll fetch you some tea in the meanwhile," suggested the Frog: "a pot of fresh lukewarm tea."

"That'd be very nice," said Alice; "only you don't have to make it lukewarm on my account, please" (for she liked tea best when it was steaming hot). The Frog, however, seemed not to hear her, and it hobbled off for the tea.

Alice had been to a country inn before, but this was the first time she had ever had the opportunity to order for herself, and it certainly was an agreeable, grown-up sensation. The only problem was that the stains on the menu card seemed to slide about so, for as soon as she found a bit that was fairly clean, and tried to read it, a stain would somehow have appeared that she knew had *not* been there before. Furthermore, they always contrived to cover the most important words, so that though she generally managed to make out what a dish was served with, or how it was prepared, she could never quite discover what it actually consisted of.

She had been studying the menu thus for a minute or two, and was feeling more and more discouraged, when a voice, quite close to her, suddenly said, "Don't you go ordering oysters, dear, whatever you do."

Alice looked up, and all round her, but there was nobody to be seen. And she was pondering this little mystery when it added, in a mournful tone, "*I* ordered oysters – and just look at me!"

"I should very much like to look at you," said Alice readily, addressing the empty seat opposite hers, which was where the voice had seemed to come from. "But I ca'n't see you at all just for the moment."

As soon as she had finished speaking, however, she heard a sort of slithering sound, and a large brown Rattle-snake slowly uncoiled itself in front of her: first, its flat smooth head emerged above the table-cloth and contemplated her through small, sad eyes; then the upper half of its body appeared, and Alice noticed that it wore a white linen napkin knotted round its – well, round itself.

She shrank back in fright (not caring greatly for snakes, as a general rule). "You needn't be afraid," said the Rattle-snake, "I wo'n't harm *you*."

"Well, I'm sure you would *mean* no harm," Alice ventured to remark, for she was always pleased to debate a point, whatever the circumstance. "The question is, would you be able to help yourself?

"What do you mean?" said the Rattle-snake.

"Just that animals ca'n't help being what they are, you know. Nor can they ever change their nature. For example, you must have heard it said that a leopard cannot change its spots."

"What nonsense!" it replied. "Most well-brought-up leopards change their spots twice a day, then change into evening spots for dinner. And no matter how hungry I get – and, goodness knows, I am awfully hungry just now – I'd never dream of eating a table companion. It simply isn't done – etiquette, you know, a sense of the social graces, and all that."

Feeling a little more at ease, Alice asked, "Have you been waiting very long, then, for your order?"

"Long enough," the Rattle-snake replied: "five weeks, four days, and two-and-a-half hours, to be precise. My mistake was ordering a dozen oysters – I'm extremely partial to oysters, you know. Only I forgot that they're to be eaten when there's an R in the month – and I've got three more weeks till that happens." And it gave a slow, drawn-out rattle, which Alice supposed was its way of sighing.

"But how are you to open them, when they do

come?" she was curious to know. "Since you don't have
– I mean, you haven't got any – "

"Fingers?" the Rattle-snake interrupted her. "That
did occur to me only the day before yesterday, but it was
too late to change the order, alas!"

"Poor dear," said Alice sympathetically, "you must
be quite starved."

"I'm so hungry," replied the Rattle-snake, " – I'm so
hungry I could eat – why, I could eat my own tail!"

As it spoke, it turned to look at its tail with a rather
unhealthy interest, Alice thought. "It does look
extremely tasty, doesn't it," the Rattle-snake went on,
its mouth beginning to water, "and if I were to wait
much longer, you know, it mightn't be so tender as it is
now."

"Please, Mr. Snake, don't do anything rash," said
Alice, who was becoming a little alarmed. "I really
ca'n't think it's such a good idea."

"What harm will just a nibble do?" said the Rattle-
snake, in an impatient tone. "Why, I doubt if I'd even
miss it."

"Oh, but do consider," Alice pleaded: "it'll be
awfully hard to judge where your tail ends and the rest
of you begins."

"It's easy, on the contrary; for my tail ends way down there and the rest of me begins right here," replied the Rattle-snake, and it tossed its head as if to demonstrate what it meant, "so there's no chance of my confusing them!"

It paid no further heed to her; but after one or two exercises to loosen up its jaws, it opened its mouth just as wide as could be and, to Alice's horror, it slowly began to swallow the tip of its tail. Further and further it advanced, and while the nether part of its body disappeared from view, what remained became plumper and plumper, so that Alice simply could not imagine where it would all end. She would have liked to try and stop it, but it had soon eaten such a lot of itself, she wouldn't even have known where to start.

Finally, the Rattle-snake had reached its own head. Making a truly heroic effort, it got its mouth wider than you would have thought it possible for any snake to do; then, with a loud, liquid snap, it swallowed that up as well! (And if you would like to see what it resembled when it had finished, look at the picture below.)

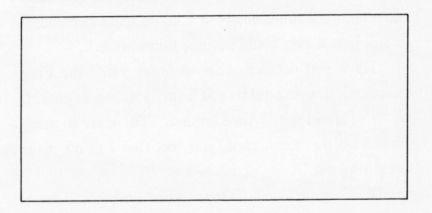

Alice sat there for a moment quite dumbfounded. Then she heard a feeble voice, which seemed to come out of the air, saying "Now that was *very* satisfying!" – followed by a ghostly rattle.

Before a few minutes had passed, the Frog-Waiter returned, bearing the tea-things on a salver.

"Here you are, Miss," it said, pouring out the tea for her. "Come, drink up."

Alice cautiously sipped the tea. "Nice and lukewarm, ain't it?" the Frog remarked, standing close by her while she tasted it. "Or perhaps you'd prefer it even lukewarmer?"

"No thank you," said Alice decidedly: "it's *quite* lukewarm enough as it is." And though she knew perfectly well how tea might be made hotter or colder, no amount of thinking about it could make her understand how it ever could become lukewarmer!

"Have you decided what to order yet?" the Frog inquired, drawing out its pad from its waistcoat pocket.

"I'm afraid not," Alice replied. "There are so many stains on the menu card, you see, that I ca'n't make anything out."

The Frog stiffened. "These 'stains', as you call them, are meant as samples, you know," it said, in an angry croak, "to show you what there is."

Alice was determined that she would not offend yet another of the creatures, so she picked up the card again and studied it as well as she could. Though it seemed a queer and not very gracious way to choose one's meal, she at last pointed to a stain whose colouring made it appear a little more appetising than the others, and said, "I think I'd like some of – of this, please."

"Swan Pie and Greens," said the Frog, looking at the stain with a nod of approval: "just what I would have ordered myself!"

Alice had never before eaten Swan Pie, but she was very fond of Pigeon Pie and Partridge Pie, and she guessed its taste must be similar. So she was not too displeased with her choice. But, instead of leaving to fetch the Pie, as she expected, the old Frog suddenly put two fingers between its lips and gave out an ear-piercing whistle. And, a moment later, a beautiful white swan which had been gliding to and fro across the placid surface of the little brook swam to the bank, climbed ashore, and waddled over to the table.

When it had come close to, however, Alice noticed that it had a grubby clay pipe in its mouth, and the first thing it did when it saw her was to take it out and scratch its head with the narrow end.

" 'Afternoon," it politely greeted her; then, inspecting her from top to toe, it added in a doubtful voice, " – though I must say, I was expecting somebody a bit bigger, like."

"Bigger?" Alice repeated. "But why?"

"Why – because *I'm* what you'd call full-grown," the Swan replied. "*Will* you be able to eat me all, that's what

I'd like to know? For I don't fancy having part of me left by the side of the plate!"

Alice tried to speak, but she could only sit and gasp. She had been told to eat all her food up many times by her nurse, but never, never by the food itself! "I promise I'll – I'll do my best," she managed to say at last.

"Well – I ca'n't ask fairer than that, can I," said the

Swan in a kindlier tone of voice. "But first off I've got to
sing my song."

"Your song?" asked Alice.

"Surely you've heard that swans always sing a song
before going into the pot?" said the Frog-Waiter.
"Why, it's a very old tradition."

"It'll be short – sweet – and at no extra charge to
you!" the Swan cheerily concluded, tapping its pipe
against the table to remove the dottle. And, as Alice
listened, it sang its song, dancing a little jig all the while:

> *"I wish I had a Mackintosh*
> *Made out of herrings' fins,*
> *Secured together, each to each,*
> *With diamond safety-pins:*
> *Then I should have no cause to fear*
> *The Seven Deadly Sins."*

The Frog took the refrain:

> *"Yes, he would have no cause to fear*
> *The Seven Deadly Sins!"*

> *"I wish I had a Thank-You Note*
> *In William Shakespeare's hand,*
> *Or Bacon's, as the case may be,*
> *Or any of that band:*
> *Then I should stick it 'neath my desk*
> *To make it upright stand."*

"Yes, he would stick it 'neath his desk
    To make it upright stand!" (And so on.)

"I wish I had an Icicle
    That echoed Big Ben's chimes,
And did not melt to H_2O
    In equatorial climes:
Then I should have good cause to write
    A letter to The Times.

I wish I had a Lawyer's Fee
    That covered every case,
The kind you buy in Regent Street
    Wrapped up in old French lace:
Then I should with impunity
    Advertisements deface.

I wish I had a Coffee Bean
    The size of Luton Hoo,
And thirty miles of Fishing-Nets,
    A Gravy-Boat or two:
Then I should – why, good gracious me,
    I don't know what I'd do!"

And the Frog came in with a final refrain:

"Yes, he would – why, good gracious me,
    I don't know what he'd do!"

When the song was over, the Swan made a little bow, and Alice thanked it very nicely for its rendition. Then, with a sigh, the Frog said, "Come on, old fellow, it's into the pot with you."

"Righty-ho!" replied the Swan, as genially as though it were being invited to go for a swim.

"Oh, please wait!" Alice interrupted, for she could not bear to think of eating somebody who had just sung to her. "Why, I – I believe, after all, I've changed my mind. I'm not really so hungry as I thought I was," she said timidly, looking now at the Frog, now at the Swan.

The Swan broke the silence first. "*There*'s gratitude for you!" it said in an indignant voice. "*No* consideration at all – and after I go to the trouble of singing her my song!"

"*And* she's scarcely touched her tea," added the Frog-Waiter, sadly shaking its head. "Such capital tea it is, too – capital tea!"

"When it says 'capital tea' like that," thought Alice to herself, "it makes it sound more like the letter than the drink. And it's a very curious notion – but all the things which have happened to me to-day seem to have been connected with letters in some way. There was the A-stack, to begin with, and the spelling bees and the sea and the Sands of Dee – and, oh, so many more! It's a pity my adventures aren't all written down in a book, for then I could turn back the pages and make certain of it. I ca'n't do *that*, of course – still, it does seem to me as if I've been travelling through the Alphabet, from A to – well, now to T." And she added thoughtfully, "I wonder if I'm right."

CHAPTER X

YOU

What do *you* think?

CHAPTER XI

THE BATTLE OF LETTERS

Alice had no more time to wonder whether she was right or not, for a cry of "The Grand Opening of Parliament! It's the Grand Opening of Parliament!" was suddenly heard in the distance. And without hesitating an instant, the Frog-Waiter seized her by the hand and began to rush off, half hopping and half running properly, a queer pace which Alice found extremely hard to keep time with. They were followed closely by the Swan, which would sometimes flap a little way into the air, in its anxiety not to be left behind.

*   *   *   *   *

*   *   *   *

*   *   *   *   *

As they approached the great Hall of Parliament, they came together with a solemn and very imposing procession, also making its way towards it, and which at first seemed to be composed of noblemen wearing splendid gold coronets and robes with rich ermine borders. But when Alice paid closer attention to them, she discovered that, underneath their regalia, they were really letters of the Alphabet.

"Look, here are the I's!" she couldn't help crying excitedly, " – and how tall and upright they are! And over there are the D's! How funny and conceited they look with their little puffed-out chests! And the F's must be dreadfully weary, or their heads wouldn't stoop so. And there are the O's – now, who is it they remind me of?" she thought to herself for a moment. "Why, Humpty Dumpty, of course!" (For it was as difficult to tell with them, as it had been with Humpty Dumpty, which was neck and which was waist.) "Don't they look comical, rolling along like that! Oh, and there's a little Q by itself – why, no, it isn't one," she corrected herself on second thoughts: "in fact, it's a cat." (Study the letter Q carefully, and you may perhaps see how the mistake was made.)

There were many other creatures too, besides the

letters, taking part in the procession – animals and birds of every kind. Even the spelling bees were there, buzzing as noisily as ever. And before she knew quite how it had happened, Alice found herself walking at the Grampus's side.

It had exchanged its professor's gown and mortar-board for a robe and a coronet, and it appeared so stately and had such a severe expression on its face, that she felt too awestruck to open the conversation. So she was not a little taken aback when, a minute later, it leant towards her to whisper in her ear, "There's absolutely nothing I like better than marching in solemn pro-cession. What a precious lark!" – and it giggled in a most *un*-solemn manner.

Soon they had arrived at the great hall, where, after the usual quarrelling over places, everybody was seated reasonably comfortably and looking in expectation at a sort of pulpit which stood on a raised platform in the middle of the floor. Alice spent these moments gazing round her: all the letters of the Alphabet seemed to be equally represented; and, packed into a narrow gallery overlooking the full length of the hall, sat the other creatures, some of which she recognised. For instance, the Country Mouse was present, poring over its

Almanac; and so were Jack and Jill (and though Jack wore a thick white bandage on his head, he was in fine fettle otherwise, so Alice felt relieved about *that*); as to the Red and White Queens, they had taken their seats on the platform, among the more august members of the company.

A short while later, six liveried ushers blew a loud fanfare on their trumpets: ⊀ ⊀ ⊀ ⊀ ⊀ ⊀ !

Everybody immediately rose to their feet. As Alice did so too, she managed to peer through the little entrance door which led into the hall, where she could observe that it was the Emu whose arrival was so keenly awaited.

"That ceiling is much too low for its height," she said to herself. "It's going to have to bend over if it wants to come in – which won't look very dignified, I think." However, as the Emu entered the hall accompanied by the Welsh Rabbit, Alice was amazed to see a large round hole suddenly form in the ceiling, one which not only accommodated its head quite easily, but actually shifted here and there in whichever direction the Emu chose to go! (And how such a thing was possible, I have *no* idea: I can only state that it was.)

When it reached the platform, it struck its gavel against the pulpit and declared the session open. Then the Welsh Rabbit came forward to make an announcement: "The main business of the day: The Emu's Constitution!"

"Oh, goody!" cried the Emu, on the point of leaving the hall again. "It's just what is needed after such a copious tea."

"No, no, your Emu-nence," the Rabbit hastily corrected it. "Not your constitutional – the Constitution. I mean that certain of the letters have been complaining of it."

"Oh, *have* they indeed?" said the Emu in a loud voice, and it peered down at the assembly through its pince-nez, causing some of those present to fidget uncomfortably. "And may I be permitted to know the nature of their complaint?" it asked.

"Lord X has the floor!" cried the Welsh Rabbit.

Everybody turned to stare at Lord X, who was very much taller than most of his fellows, being what we would call a capital X. He rose clutching a sheaf of papers, which, even at the distance she was sitting, Alice could see were in complete disorder. Shuffling and re-shuffling them several times, he noisily cleared his throat and spoke at last.

"*Why* – " he began in a booming voice; then he left off, but whether it was from a desire to make a dramatic effect (which he certainly achieved), or because his papers were still not sorted out, was at first unclear. By stretching forward, however, Alice was able to note to her amusement that each sheet of paper had but a single word written on it, "and so that's the reason he ca'n't complete his question!"

"*Why*, I – I ask you – " Lord X stammered, then began to search frantically among his papers for the next word.

"I fear this may be *very* tedious," the Grampus whispered to Alice.

"I'm sure it will be," she replied, also in a low voice, "unless he manages to put his papers in order."

"It's not what I mean, child," the Grampus went on. "You see, I have proved conclusively, by Algebra, that if Lord X starts his speech by asking Why, he must end by putting us all to sleep. I sha'n't trouble you with the working-out, which as you can imagine is of the utmost complication, but you shall see the result for yourself" – and it drew out its album, which it had concealed within the folds of its robe, and held a page open to show Alice. It was full of calculations and lots of scorings out, but at the bottom she could read the equation which the Grampus had arrived at: "$X + Y = ZZZZZ$. Q.E.D." And, to be sure, it did appear to be the correct answer, for a number of the letters were already beginning to doze off: the C's and the O's were the very worst offenders, no doubt because they had nice soft shoulders against which they could cosily curl up together, "just like white mice in a cage," thought Alice. A few of the younger O's, however, had propped up their writing slates on the bench and were quietly enjoying a game of Noughts and Crosses with a little group of neighbouring X's.

Suddenly, unable to prevent himself, one of the Y's gave out such a yawn that, of course, all the others were immediately infected, and it proceeded to spread from letter to letter right through the room.

"Arrest that yawn!" shrieked the Emu. "Turn it out! Clap it in irons! Feed it nothing but bread and water!"

For some minutes, the whole assembly was in turmoil, while everybody yawned away madly, and the Welsh Rabbit scurried out, returning almost at once carrying a large mirror. Without pausing for breath, it ran over to the latest victim, a very swollen-looking O, held the mirror up in front of him, and neatly trapped the yawn inside the reflection. ("I must remember that trick," said Alice to herself, "the next time I am caught with a yawning fit.")

Because of this confusion, Lord X had finally got his papers in good order and was ready to begin his speech. "*Why*, I ask you," he cried, raising his arms in supplication: "why must such fine, upstanding letters of the Alphabet as V, W, X, Y and Z – " (at this the hall broke into mixed cheering and booing, and Alice recalled reading about the same kind of behaviour taking place in the British Parliament) " – always suffer because of our position in the scheme of things? Why, I ask you once more, must we always come *last*?"

There was a cry of "Hear, hear!" from the gallery, and Alice was sure she recognised the voice of the Crocodile.

"I therefore propose," Lord X continued, "that our glorious Alphabet would be even Alpha*better* if, instead of speaking about our ABC, we henceforth spoke about our XYZ!"

"Stuff and nonsense!" screamed an excitable C, whose curve was swiftly flattened out when a nearby Z sat upon him.

"For is it not monstrously unjust," said Lord X, glaring through his monocle at what remained of the poor little C, "that we only serve for useless words like 'verbosity' and 'xylograph' and 'zygoma'? Why, it's only – "

But he was interrupted again. "As long as *you* are in full flight, X," an A pointedly called out, "there'll always be a use for 'verbosity'!"

"*I say*, it's only out of charity to us," Lord X persisted, "that such words are put into the dictionary at all!"

"That isn't so," Alice whispered to the Grampus.

"It's not the reason for any words being in the dictionary."

"Oh, my dear," replied the Grampus with a frown, "what else do you expect from a Parliament? After all, it's in the root of the word – and the thing too, alas."

"What do you mean?" asked Alice.

"Well, ca'n't you see," the Grampus explained: " 'Parliament' comes from the French *'parlement'*: *'parle'* from the word *'parler'* – 'to speak', and *'ment'* from the word *'mentir'* – 'to lie'. They all do tell lies, you know."

Alice did not know, but she could not help wondering if it might be true.

Meanwhile tempers had already started to rise in an alarming way. A young E jumped up from the back benches. "At least you're only obliged to work part-time!" he shouted at the X's. "It's not a twenty-four-hours-a-day job like ours!"

"That's well said!" one of his neighbours agreed. "Why, every other word seems to need an E – sometimes *two*! There are days when I'm quite worked off my feet!"

"You haven't any," an X shouted back, "so stop complaining!"

"I did have – till I was worked off 'em," the E sulkily replied.

"E's right!" a tall, angular A cried out. "And what's more, all the really interesting words are allotted to X, Y and Z! We have to take what we get – and no talking back!"

"But *we're* always kept waiting to the very end," grumbled a W (who, of course, required *two* places on the bench). "Yesterday, for instance, the tea-tray took so long to reach us my tea was stone cold."

"Not so! Not so!" spoke up one of the T's. "We're just as warm with you as with any of the other letters!"

"With *U* perhaps – but not with *W*!" replied the latter with a sneer. Whereupon all his fellow W's clapped their hands in delight that he had made such a clever riposte.

"Well, speaking for myself, *my* Hot Cross Bun was cold last Easter," an F ventured to say, so sleepily, however, that he did not even bother to lift his head.

"Why, of all the –" spluttered the X who had spoken before. "It's just because you F's are so slow at everything, that it gets cold!"

"Oho, who's complaining now?" the E asked triumphantly.

"E can talk," a rather melancholy V came in. "Think how many words there are in which he's allowed another E to keep company with him. Whoever saw two V's together in the same word? Nobody realises what a lonely life a V has!" – and a tear slowly rolled down his left-hand side, and trembled upon his lowermost point for what seemed an eternity before dropping off at last, so that (as Alice afterwards described it) "he looked just like the melting tip of an icicle."

"And a W!"

"And an X!"

"And a Y!"

"And a Z!"

As the Grampus listened to the arguments, the expression on its face became more and more preoccupied. "I don't like the look of it," it could be heard muttering, "I don't like the look of it at all." Then, clutching its Auto-biography, it hurriedly began to slide under the bench.

Indeed, thought Alice, the atmosphere in the hall was turning *very* ominous. "It's almost as if – " she began to say – when, in a flash, battle was joined. First into the fray were the A's and the V's. They lunged out at each other, pointed edges to the fore, reminding Alice of some pictures she had chanced to see in one of her cousin's books, of Knights jousting in mediaeval tournaments. Then the K's started to snap at everything in sight with their sharp little jaws. The O's propelled themselves across the room like cannonballs, making a strange humming noise as they flew by. And the E's and I's combined forces by changing into tridents and puncturing all those letters, like the C's and G's and U's, whose soft curves made them vulnerable to their attack.

Everything seemed to go mad at once. The Welsh Rabbit somehow managed to squeeze inside its own bottle of Worcestershire Sauce, so that you could see its eyes peering out fearfully from behind the label; the Emu crazily set about hammering itself into the ground with its gavel; and the two Queens, began to run round and round together in dizzying circles, as though each were the other's tail, which she was chasing, and the White Queen's hair was all awry, and the Red Queen was screaming a queer little song at her, whose words Alice could just about make out above the general din:

> "*Gather ye hair-pins while ye may:*
> *The rude West Wind is blowing;*
> *And these same curls that to to-day*
> *To-morrow will be fro-ing!*"

Alice watched them all for a few minutes; and, really, the confusion was such, that she could not help laughing out loud. Boldly, she stood up (discovering to her surprise that she was now close to her proper height), and cried out, "Oh, you are all so silly! For you know you are nothing but the servants of words, which are the servants of the people who use them!"

In an instant the fighting ceased. But instead of

making peace with each other, as she hoped, the letters all turned to face Alice. Slowly they advanced, A's, B's and C's side by side with X's, Y's and Z's, united now against a common enemy.

Alice did not know whether to be amused or frightened: but, just in case it ought to be the latter, she quickly searched in her pocket for a weapon, however small, which she could use to beat them off – when suddenly, led by a particularly sharp A, the whole Alphabet flew up and straight upon her! "AAAAA

CHAPTER XII

WAS IT A DREAM?

AAAAAH!'' – Alice gave out a shrill little scream, for she thought she felt the A's sharp point pricking her; and it did appear to be so, as, immediately after, a tiny drop of blood had formed on the tip of her thumb. "Why, that bad-tempered A – I'll – I'll –'' she started to say angrily, when she realised, looking down, that what had drawn blood was not the A at all, but her own needle, which she was holding in her right hand along with the thread in her left. Alice sat up, rubbed her eyes, and looked round her. She was once more – I mean, she was *still* – curled up by the roaring fire and, in front of her, Dinah was sleeping peacefully on the rug. Nothing had changed from when she last saw it. Even the sand in the hour-glass, which Alice could remember turning upside-down only a few minutes before all her adventures began, was just as it had been: a grain or two had fallen from the upper globe into the lower one, perhaps, but no more, as far as Alice could make out.

"So it was only a dream," she mused, gently stroking Dinah, who twitched in her sleep as if she, too, were having an exciting dream. "And what can *yours* be like?" Alice wondered. "Nothing at all like mine, I'm certain," she said, as she gazed fondly at the little bundle of living fur: "because, you darling, though you might easily want to dream about the Country Mouse – oh yes, I know, only to gobble it right up – you'd be *very* puzzled by the Emu, and the Grampus with its Autobiography, and Jack and Jill, and the two Queens who dropped in from another dream to keep me company, and all the other strange creatures I met!"

Alice sighed, almost in disappointment that she had not really met them, even if, just for the moment, they seemed quite real to her. "Yes, dear, only a dream – a dream in Alphabetical Order – " she went on, addressing Dinah yet speaking very softly so as not to wake her (which is in the logic of a little child), " – from A, which stands for me, don't you see, A as in Alice – to Z, which must mean your snoring, I'm afraid."

Then suddenly she heard a more pronounced noise – zzzzz – from somewhere in the room. It seemed to come from the window, and she got up and hurried over to investigate what it might be; and what was her astonishment to discover a bee buzzing against the window-pane.

"Why then," said Alice excitedly, opening the latch to let it free, "perhaps after all it wasn't a dream – perhaps it really *did* happen to me! This *must* be one of the spelling bees, for where we are now, it's December, you know," she went on, half to herself and half to uncaring Dinah, "and you never find a bee in the month of December!"

Oh but you are nodding, child: or else, it is high time you brushed up your spelling. For of course there's a 'b' in 'December'!

HOW THIS BOOK CAME
TO BE WRITTEN

(It happened that the Author was walking in the Quantocks, a range of hills in Somerset remarkable for its power of echo, where he was reflecting upon the proximity of middle-age.)

"What must we feel when, in the glass
Of Time's resistless flow,
We watch the measured grains of sand
(That e'er more swiftly go)
Deplete the globe of Years To Come
And swell its twin below?"

The echo came: "Be low!"

"Yet twice in Years Gone By we could
These nameless fears surpass –
When Alice walked in Wonderland
And through the Looking-Glass.
How sad no third *adventure lies*
In wait for such a lass!"

The echo came: "Alas!"

"Oh, echo, do we not both yield
To premature despair?
Might someone not present himself
As Lewis Carroll's heir?
But oh! who would this role assume,
If only as a dare?"

The echo came: "Adair!"